FALLING FOR THE REBEL FALCON

BY
LUCY GORDON

MILLS
BOON

First published in Great Britain 2013
by Mills & Boon, an imprint of Harlequin (UK) Limited.
Harlequin (UK) Limited, Eton House, 18-24 Paradise Road,
Richmond, Surrey TW9 1SR

© Lucy Gordon 2013

ISBN: 978 0 263 23494 7

Harlequin (UK) policy is to use papers that are natural, renewable and recyclable products and made from wood grown in sustainable forests. The logging and manufacturing process conform to the legal environmental regulations of the country of origin.

Printed and bound in Great Britain
by CPI Antony Rowe, Chippenham, Wiltshire

Lucy Gordon cut her writing teeth on magazine journalism, interviewing many of the world's most interesting men, including Warren Beatty, Charlton Heston and Roger Moore. She also camped out with lions in Africa, and had many other unusual experiences, which have often provided the background for her books. Several years ago, while staying in Venice, she met a Venetian who proposed in two days. They have been married ever since. Naturally this has affected her writing, where romantic Italian men tend to feature strongly.

Two of her books have won a Romance Writers of America RITA® Award.

You can visit her website at www.lucy-gordon.com

Books by Lucy Gordon:

THE SECRET THAT CHANGED EVERYTHING
PLAIN JANE IN THE SPOTLIGHT*
MISS PRIM AND THE BILLIONAIRE*
RESCUED BY THE BROODING TYCOON*
HIS DIAMOND BRIDE
A WINTER PROPOSAL

*The Falcon Dynasty

I dedicate this book to Katerina, my friend in Russia, who has told me so much about that lovely country.

PROLOGUE

'*DON'T LEAVE ME. Please, please don't leave me!*'

Varushka's voice rose to a desperate cry. She reached out frantically, seeking someone who wasn't there, who hadn't been there for many years, who would never be there.

'Where are you? Come back! *Don't leave me!*'

She cried out again and again, then gasped as she felt a pair of loving arms enfold her.

'I'm here, Mamma. I haven't gone anywhere.'

The young man's voice was affectionate and comforting, but it hardly seemed to reach the middle-aged woman sitting on the garden seat. Her eyes were closed, seeming to lock her into the prison of her private misery.

'Don't go,' she whispered. 'Stay with me. I beg you.'

'Mamma, wake up, please.' The young man sounded distraught. 'It's me, Leonid, your son. I'm not…anyone else. Open your eyes. Look at me.'

He moved closer beside her on the garden seat, touching her face with gentle fingers to brush away the tears.

'Open your eyes,' he begged again.

She did so, but stared in bewilderment, as though unable to recognise him. His heart sank, and for a moment he too was on the verge of weeping. Determinedly he controlled the weakness.

'Mamma,' he murmured. *'Please.'*

At last the vacant look died out of her eyes, and she managed a feeble smile as she finally recognised her son.

'Forgive me,' she murmured. 'I fell asleep, and in my dreams *he* was there with me. I felt his hands taking hold of me—'

'They were my hands, Mamma,' Leonid said gently. 'I came out to find you here in the garden to say goodbye. I'm off to attend Marcel's wedding in Paris. Didn't you remember that I said I was leaving today?'

'Yes,' she sighed. 'Of course I remembered.'

But they both knew it wasn't his departure that had made her cry out in terrible anguish, but another departure long ago; and the memory of a man who'd vowed to return, but who had done so only rarely over thirty years, and never for long.

'Naturally you must go now,' she said. 'Your father will be waiting for you in Paris. Oh, how he'll be longing to see you!'

If he was there at all, Leonid thought. With another man it could be taken for granted that he would attend the wedding of one of his sons, but with Amos Falcon nothing could be taken for granted.

'You've got my letter?' Varushka urged. 'You'll give it to him?'

'Of course I will, Mamma.'

'And you'll bring his letter back to me?'

'I promise.'

Even if I have to twist his arm to make him write something, he brooded. But she must not be allowed to suspect his thoughts.

'Perhaps he might even come back with you,' she murmured. 'Oh yes, say that you'll bring him here to see me. Promise me.'

'I can't promise, Mamma,' he said. 'He has so many demands on his time, and Marcel's wedding cropped up so suddenly that he couldn't make any plans.'

'But you will try? Tell him how much I long to see him, and I know that will make him decide.'

'I'll do my best,' he said, speaking with difficulty. 'Perhaps you should come into the house now. It's getting chilly.'

'Let me stay here. I love looking at this so much.' She made a gesture towards the lawn that sloped down and away, giving them a splendid view of the Don River. 'It's where we were together, where we will one day be together again. I know that. I must simply be patient. Goodbye, my dear boy. I'll wait to hear from you.'

He drew her close in a hug, kissed her lovingly then walked away with a heavy heart.

As he neared the house he saw an elderly woman watching him through a window. She was Nina, who looked after his mother, and who now came to the door.

'How is she managing?'

'Not well,' he sighed. 'She's given me a letter for my father. It's sad that she still believes he loves her after all these years.'

'Whereas Amos Falcon used her, abandoned her, broke every promise he ever made to her,' Nina said scathingly. Although, strictly speaking, she was Leonid's employee, she knew she could risk talking like this of his father. He treasured her for his mother's sake, and it was only because he trusted Nina to care for her that he was able to leave this country house and return to Moscow, where he had to live for the sake of his extensive business interests.

'He didn't break every promise,' he reminded her. 'He's supported Mamma financially—'

'From a distance. That was easy for him. Where was

he when her husband learned he wasn't your father? Did he offer to help, except with cash?'

'I suffer for her as much as you do, Nina. When I see him in Paris I'm going to do my best.'

'Can you get him to come here for a visit? You know she's set her heart on that?'

'Yes. I'll try.' He gave a soft groan. 'What can I do? She lives in a fantasy world in which he loves her and will one day return. Is it better for her to believe those dreams than face the truth?'

'Let her believe them if it helps her endure life,' Nina advised.

'You're right. I must go now.' He squeezed her hand. 'What would I do without you?'

'You don't have to. I'm going into the garden now so that she won't be alone as you go. Be off now or you'll miss your plane.'

He went down to where a man was waiting with the car. At the last minute he turned to look up the sloping lawn to where his mother was waving. He blew kisses, giving her his brightest smile so that she wouldn't suspect the sadness that overtook him at the thought of her bleak life.

It would never improve, he knew. He could only do his best to make her remaining time as contented as possible. But it wasn't in his power to give her the happiness she craved.

Varushka watched the car as it vanished into the distance.

'Oh Nina, it's so wonderful,' she said. 'He's going to see his father in Paris, and bring Amos back to see me.'

'If he can,' Nina said carefully.

'Oh yes, he will. He said Amos would definitely return to see me in a few days.' She sighed ecstatically. 'He gave me his promise.'

CHAPTER ONE

PERDITA GUESSED WHO was here as soon as she heard the frenzied knock on her door. Sure enough, it was Jim, a nice young man who considered himself her boyfriend, standing there, agitated.

'Perdita, you can't do this to me. It's not fair.'

'Hush, don't shout. Come inside.'

He came rushing in and threw himself onto the sofa, growling, 'How do you expect me to feel when I've been looking forward to our time together and you dump me?' He held up his cellphone. 'By text, for Pete's sake!'

'I didn't dump you, I just said I can't get away for our little trip next week. Something's come up. I'm sorry, Jim. I'll make it up to you another time.'

She spoke sweetly but Jim wasn't placated. Perdita Davis was a little too good at this, winning a man's heart, backing off then soothing him with a beguiling smile.

She could get away with it because she was gorgeous, with long blonde hair, devastating blue eyes, a figure slender enough for the most demanding clothes and a lot of impish charm. That was the trouble, he thought crossly. She knew exactly how far she could go.

'I have to dash off soon,' she said. 'There's a story coming up that I just can't miss.'

Perdita was a freelance journalist with a talent for dis-
covering scoops and exploiting them to the full.

'So where is this earth-shattering story?' Jim seethed.

'Paris. I've just booked my room at La Couronne.'

'That's the most expensive hotel in Paris.'

'I know. I managed to get the very last room. It's been
filling up fast since the rumours started.'

'What rumours?'

'The wedding. Marcel Falcon is getting married in a
few days.'

'And who the blazes is Marcel Falcon?'

'He's the owner of La Couronne, but that's not the point.
His half-brother is Travis Falcon. You must have heard of
him, surely?'

'Sure. Big TV star.'

'He's been in the news a lot recently because of this new
woman in his life. Apparently she's not like the slinky,
sexy "bits of fun" he's usually seen with. She's actually
respectable, and everyone's dying to see how it will turn
out. My contact in Paris says Travis will be at the wedding, and she'll be with him. I've simply got to be there
and get close enough to see them together. Plus, of course,
all the others.'

'What others?'

'The rest of the Falcon family. The father is Amos Falcon, a big noise in financial circles. He'll almost certainly
be in Paris. And so will his other sons.'

'How many has he got?'

'Five. By four different mothers. There's Darius, who's
English and also a big noise financially. His brother Jackson, who does those television documentaries. Marcel,
who's French, Travis, who's American, and Leonid, Russian.'

'All those nationalities? Amos Falcon gets around, doesn't he?'

'He did once. He's in his seventies now and he lives in Monaco with his most recent wife. He seems respectable but I'll bet he isn't really. The leopard doesn't change its spots.'

'But the place will be bulging with press. Why bother when you'll just be one of a crowd?'

She gave him an ironic glance which told him exactly what he could do with that idea. Perdita was never simply one of a crowd.

'They're not marrying in a public church,' she said. 'La Couronne has its own chapel, so they can control who gets in. The press will be kept at a distance. That's why I need to be in the hotel as a guest. If I play my cards right I might even get invited to the wedding.'

Jim gave a hoot of laughter. 'In your dreams! You might contrive to sneak in, but even you couldn't manage to get invited.'

'Wanna bet?'

'No, I guess you could do it if anyone could. You know, one day you'll meet a guy who'll play you at your own game.'

'Nobody knows what my game is,' she pointed out, all wide-eyed innocence.

'He will. Then you'll be sorry.'

'Maybe. Or maybe I'll end up enjoying it. The more of a battle there is, the more fun it is to win.'

She'd said everything, Jim realised. Whoever could beat her at her own game, it wouldn't be himself. She'd told him that, kindly but finally.

'What time's your flight?' he asked.

'Three hours. I was just about to call a taxi.'

'No need. I'll take you to the airport.'

'Oh Jim, that's so nice of you. How can any man be so sweet and forgiving?'

Good question, he thought wryly. Despite being aggrieved at how little he mattered to her, he still found himself eager to serve her.

But that was Perdita, he sighed. She could have that effect on a man.

He carried her bags down to the car, made sure she was comfortable, and headed for the airport.

'If this wedding's being kept under wraps, how come you found out?' he asked when they were halfway there.

'I got a tip-off from someone who owed me a favour.'

He should have known. That too was Perdita's way. There was always someone who owed her a favour.

At the airport he saw her to Check-In and was rewarded by a peck on the cheek.

'Thank you, Jim dear. I'll be in touch.'

But she didn't say when, he noticed. She would have forgotten him by the time she was in her seat.

Here he did Perdita an injustice. She was sorry to have hurt Jim, however unintentionally, and thought about him until the plane was in the air. Only then did she turn her mind to the job she was about to do.

It was nearly midnight when they reached Charles de Gaulle Airport, and she emerged from Customs to find a middle-aged woman waiting for her. This was Hortense, a French businesswoman with extensive contacts. She and Perdita liked each other, and also had a flourishing business relationship based on the exchange of favours. After enthusiastic greetings they headed for the car.

'I don't know how to thank you,' Perdita said as they made their way towards Paris.

'No need. I owed you. It was just a lucky chance. The company I work for is organising the wedding.'

'Why is it all being done so hurriedly?'

'Rumour says Marcel is afraid of losing Cassie. When she agreed to marry him he moved fast before she could change her mind.'

'What about the family?'

'They should be here tomorrow. Travis from Los Angeles, Darius and Jackson from England. Perhaps even Leonid from Russia. He's got a room booked but nobody's sure if he'll actually come. People who know him say he's hard as nails. You cross him at your peril.'

'Hmm. He sounds interesting.'

'Dangerous. If you meet him, be careful.'

'But why? Where's the fun in being careful?'

'Must everything in life be fun?'

'Of course. Fun is good. Fun is creative. Fun puts you in control and catches *him* on the wrong foot.'

'Him? Who him?'

'Any him.'

'And that's important?'

'Oh yes,' Perdita said with a little smile. 'That's very important.'

Hortense made no reply. It could be hard to know just how much of Perdita's lively speech she actually meant.

They had reached the most expensive part of Paris, and soon a magnificent building reared up before them.

'There's La Couronne,' Hortense said.

'Wow! It looks a fabulous place.'

'It was once the home of aristocrats, but the family was wiped out in the French Revolution, and the building went into decline until Marcel bought it. He specialises in grandiose hotels in big cities all over the world, and La Couronne is the best.'

When she'd checked in Hortense accompanied her upstairs to her room, whose luxury made Perdita nod appreciatively.

'It may strain your budget,' Hortense said, 'but it was the last one available, and it's on the same corridor as the Falcons.'

'That's the bit that matters,' Perdita agreed.

They ordered a meal from Room Service and sat munching contentedly.

'Was it difficult to dash off at a moment's notice?' Hortense asked.

'Well, one person wasn't too happy,' Perdita admitted, and told her about Jim.

'But in another way it was handy,' she added. 'I was due to go to my parents tomorrow, for a party to celebrate my cousin Sally's engagement, and it's probably better that I won't be there.'

'Your parents are academics, aren't they? Big names in the world of learning, so I've heard.'

It was true that Professor Angus Hanson was an imposing man whose learning and reputation struck awe into the hearts of those who knew him. His family were equally erudite, occupying high positions in research and education. All except Perdita, his youngest child.

'They've always seen me as the black sheep,' she told Hortense. 'Frivolous, foolish, not caring about serious matters.'

'Why is it better that you're not there?'

'Sally's fiancé is a man I used to know, about three years ago. It seemed to be going well for us, but then I got the chance of a big scoop. Someone let slip something. I followed it up and…well, it did me a lot of good professionally.'

'Ah yes, I remember hearing about that. It made your reputation as a journalist.'

'But Thomas was horrified. He thought it was all terribly vulgar, and wanted me to abandon my career. When I wouldn't...well...' She shrugged.

'If he'd loved you he wouldn't have broken your heart for a reason like that,' Hortense said, shocked.

'Who said my heart was broken?' Perdita demanded indignantly. 'With all the chances that were opening up for me, I had other things to think of. Besides, I realised that he didn't love me. He's an academic, and he wanted to join my family for the sake of their standing.'

'So he courted your cousin instead. Yes, it's better you're not at their engagement party.'

Perdita gave a wry smile. 'The only thing academic about me is my name. Apparently when my father discovered that my mother was pregnant yet again he groaned, "Well, I'll go to perdition!"'

'And perdition means hell, doesn't it?' Hortense chuckled.

'That's right. He really wasn't keen on another child. After that, Perdita became the family nickname for me.'

'But it's not really your name, is it?' Hortense said. 'You write your features as Perdita Davis, but I noticed you checked in as Erica Hanson.'

'Yes, that's my real name, but I only use it for official stuff. Erica Hanson keeps her bank account in order, pays her taxes on time and generally behaves properly. Perdita Davis is as foolish and frivolous as a scholarly family ever produced.'

She said this with an air of pleasure, even pride.

'Where does the Davis name come from?'

'The family more or less ordered me not to use Hanson in case people connected me with them and they died of shame,' Perdita said ironically. 'I just plucked Davis out of the air.'

'So they can deny all knowledge of you,' Hortense said, outraged. 'That's pretty nasty of them.'

'They have a serious reputation to keep up,' Perdita said, shrugging. 'You can't really blame them.'

'I can. Reputation nothing! You're a big success but they treat you like an outcast.'

'Oh, I'm not melodramatic about it,' Perdita said. 'It's not really important.'

She spoke lightly to hide the fact that Hortense had hit a nerve. In truth she cared more for her family's attitude than she would admit, and her friend's indignation on her behalf warmed her heart.

'They're probably jealous that you're making your fortune out of it,' Hortense observed. 'Your scoops are fast taking you to the top. Though, let's face it, you do sometimes sail a bit close to the edge.'

'I did at one time,' Perdita agreed. 'But recently I've been a bit less "adventurous". I don't break quite so many rules now. I'm even getting a bit respectable.'

'You?'

Perdita shrugged. 'Maybe it's my academic background coming out at last. Serious, respectable, upright. How about that?'

'What brought this about?'

'There was a big commotion recently. Have you ever heard of—?' She named a journalist so notorious that his name was known over many countries.

'Yes, wasn't he the one who tricked that woman into talking to him, and it all ended in tragedy?'

'That's right.'

'But surely it had nothing to do with you?'

'No, I wasn't involved in any way. But I met him once a few years back, and vaguely admired his tricksy methods. Not now, though. Let's say I've grown up a bit, and it made me think about the road I was travelling.'

'Does that mean strait-laced Erica has taken over completely, and cheeky Perdita no longer exists?'

'Not at all. Perdita's still there, still maddening, still taking chances. But these days she's a bit more careful about how she might affect other people.'

Hortense chuckled. 'Serve you right if you met the man of your dreams and had to choose between your two selves. That would teach you a lesson.'

'I don't have any dreams,' Perdita said cheekily. 'My heart's never been broken and it's never going to be. I've got too many other things to do.'

'Have you no sense of romance?' Hortense demanded indignantly. 'Here you are in Paris, the most romantic city in the world, and you're not entranced the way any other woman would be.'

'When I get my scoop I'll be entranced.'

'I know better than to argue with that. I'll be off to my own room, we have a busy day tomorrow. Goodnight. See you at breakfast.'

When she was alone Perdita went to the window, looking out to where the Eiffel Tower glowed in the distance. Everything in her surroundings was glamorous, and that was just how she liked it. It emphasised the life she wanted and the way she liked to see herself.

She'd told Hortense that her heart had never been broken and it was almost true.

After the riotous success that had made Thomas run from her she'd gone from strength to strength. The life of a freelancer suited her perfectly because it made her the one in charge, choosing her own targets.

Then she'd met Frank, a photographer. They'd worked as a team and she'd fallen in love with him, although these days she denied, it even to herself. But he'd betrayed her, using her talents to get close to a notorious story, then selling his pictures to another journalist who could do more for his career.

After that she'd decided to work alone, taking her own pictures. She'd learned a lot of technique from Frank, so who needed photographers? If it came to that, who needed men?

'Maybe there's something wrong with me, always putting the job first,' she mused. 'But that's the way I am. It's not my fault if I like fun. And fun likes me. Ah well! Time for bed.'

Next morning Hortense dropped in to Perdita's room just as she was getting up.

'Sorry to arrive so early,' she said, 'but I've got a busy day ahead preparing for this wedding.'

'No problem.' Perdita lifted the phone. 'Let's have some breakfast.'

While they waited for the food to arrive she took a shower, then sat in a bathrobe to eat, seizing the chance to ask more about the Falcon family.

'I don't really know anything about Leonid,' she said. 'He isn't as easy to research as the others.'

'True. His real name isn't even Falcon. He's actually Leonid Tsarev. It's only when he's over here with his brothers that he's called Falcon as a courtesy. All anyone really knows about him is that he's an incredibly successful business magnate—they call them oligarchs in Russia, don't they? I've got friends in Moscow who say he doesn't seem to have a very interesting private life. All work and money, no time for pleasure. At least, not the kind of pleasure the world hears about, if you know what I mean. Grim and gruff.'

'They can be interesting too,' Perdita mused. 'Now, what am I going to wear today?'

'Let's look,' Hortense said, opening the wardrobe. 'Hey, what lovely clothes you've got. You must have a very rich boyfriend.'

'Well, I don't. I pay for my own clothes.'

'You must be making a fortune.'

'I do all right, but I don't usually buy such expensive things. I splashed out a bit to come to this hotel. I wanted to look as if I fit in with the millionaires.'

'You'll do that all right.' She pulled down pair of luxurious stretch jeans. 'You can actually get into these?'

'Sure.'

Hortense held them up against her plump figure, and sighed. 'You know, I could murder you for being slim enough for these. Hey ho!' She tossed them onto the bed. 'Put them on.'

'But do I want to wear them right now?' Perdita mused. 'I'd like to give a first impression of severe, virtuous modesty. Maybe even a bit dull.'

'In your dreams! Listen, if a kindly fate has made you slim enough to wear these, count your blessings. Who knows how long those blessings will last? Right, now I've got to be going. And remember, if we happen to bump into each other—'

'We've never met before,' Perdita vowed.

'Thanks. If they knew I'd been in touch with a journalist I'd be in trouble. They're very sniffy about that. Bye.'

When she was alone Perdita eyed several garments, before deciding that she would, after all, wear the snug-fitting jeans. In contrast with their provocation she chose a loose blouse of white silk, that came modestly halfway down her thighs. It was good to be elegant and expensive, but nobody could accuse her of flaunting herself.

She headed out and began wandering around the hotel, studying, listening, taking photographs with her discreet camera, whose tiny size belied its power. Gradually she saw members of the Falcon family, but as yet no sign of the one she wanted.

Then, as she came to the top of a grand staircase, she paused and drew back, wondering if she could really see what she thought she could. At the foot of the stairs was a man whose height, dark hair and handsome features suggested that her search was over. Travis Falcon. This must be him. She was too far away to make out details, but what she could see was surely Travis.

There was no sign of the woman he was supposed to be bringing with him. That could be helpful, if only she could get him alone for a while.

But how to make him notice her, chat for a moment? It wouldn't be easy.

'But I think I see a way,' she murmured.

She had perfected a technique for this kind of occasion. Moving carefully, she could appear to slip on the stairs, creating just enough commotion to attract attention. Quietly she crept down the stairs, not to alert him. Only when she was three steps up did she seem to collapse, rolling down to the bottom.

At once she knew that she'd done something wrong. Instead of the easy landing she'd planned, she felt a sharp pain go through her ankle as her foot twisted beneath her. Wildly she grabbed at the banister and came to a sudden halt at his feet, so that he nearly tripped over her.

He made an explosive sound and dropped to his knees, reaching out both hands to support her, making an explosive sound, then demanding in French, *'Que le diable? Êtes-vous blessé?'*

'I don't understand—' she gasped.

'Are you hurt?' he repeated in English.

'I...I'm not sure,' she gasped, wincing from the pain. 'My ankle—'

'Have you twisted it?'

'I think so—*aaah!*'

Still holding one of her hands, he put his other arm about her and drew her to her feet.

'Try to put your weight on it,' he said. 'Just very gently.'

She tried but gave up at once. She would have fallen but for the strength of his arm about her waist, keeping her safe. She raised her eyes to his face.

It was the wrong face.

This man looked enough like Travis Falcon to be mistaken for him at a distance, but up close there was no chance.

'Oh!' she gasped before she could stop herself.

'I think you need a doctor,' he said in an accented voice that confirmed her fears. Travis was American. This man came from Eastern Europe.

'No, I can manage,' she said hastily.

'I don't think you can. Let's collect your things before you lose them.'

She supported herself by clinging to the banister while he scooped up her purse and several papers that had fallen onto the floor from her bag.

'One of them's your passport,' he said. 'You should take better care of it. What room are you in?' She gave him the number. 'Right, put your arms around my neck.'

She did so and he reached down to lift her very slowly and carefully.

'Is that all right?' he asked. 'I'm not hurting you, am I?'

'No, I'm fine.'

'Then let's go.'

Turning, he climbed the stairs to the top, then headed

down the corridor to her room. She reached into her bag for the key and he carried her inside, laying her down gently on the bed.

'All right?' he asked anxiously.

'Yes, I'm not really hurt.'

'We'll see what the doctor says about that.' Without seeking her consent, he took up the phone and called the management.

'I need a doctor here at once to look after a woman who tripped on the stairs.' He gave the room number and hung up. 'They're sending someone at once.'

'You're very kind.'

'Not at all. I'm really trying to ease my own mind. When I heard you behind me I turned sharply, and I hate to think I caused you to trip.'

She knew a moment's self-reproach that he should blame himself for the fall she had contrived. But there was something pleasant and comforting about his determination to care for her. She'd always prided herself on being self-sufficient, independent. In her job these were necessary virtues. But it was nice to be looked after, just for a few minutes.

'While we wait for the doctor I will order you a hot drink,' he said. 'Tea? Coffee?'

'Tea, thank you.'

When he'd telephoned the order he turned back to Perdita and studied her closely, frowning, almost scowling. Now she saw that he was mopping the front of his suit where something had been spilled.

'Did I do that?' she asked.

'Unfortunately I happened to be carrying a small glass of wine. Don't worry. Accidents happen. It's not as if you fell on purpose.'

'No,' she said with a twinge of guilt. 'I'm sorry to have troubled you.'

'It seems to be me who troubled you. Why did the sight of me give you such a nasty shock?' He gave her a flinty stare. 'Let me guess. You thought I was Travis, didn't you?'

'I…no, I…it wasn't…I don't understand. Travis?'

'Travis Falcon.'

'Oh yes,' she said vaguely. 'He's on television, isn't he?'

'That's putting it mildly. Apparently we look very much alike. People often think they're meeting him and are disappointed when it's only me.'

'How rude of them! Are you related?'

'He's my half-brother. My name is Leonid Tsarev.'

He extended his hand and she shook it, trying to control her whirling thoughts. She was shocked at herself. She, who prided herself on being in command of every situation, was suddenly reduced to stammering confusion.

'How…how do you do?' she murmured.

CHAPTER TWO

'I COULD ASK you the same,' he said wryly, 'but it's a silly question. Neither of us seems to be doing very well since meeting the other.'

'I guess you're right. Ouch!' She reached down to her ankle, which had hurt as she moved it.

'The doctor will be here soon,' he said. 'He can make a full assessment.'

'I hope so,' she said, rubbing the spot, but making little impact because the material of the jeans was in the way.

'You'll need to take them off so that the doctor can get to it,' Leonid said. 'Ah, there's someone at the door.'

While he went to the door she started to undress, meaning to pull the sheets over her, to preserve modesty. First she removed her right shoe, then tried to remove her left, but this was the injured foot and pulling at the shoe was intensely painful. She was still floundering when he turned back into the room, carrying a tray of tea.

'Are you having trouble?' he asked, quickly setting down the tray.

'Yes, this shoe won't move—*ow!*'

He set down the tray. 'Let me help you. Just lie there and I'll do the work.'

He eased the shoe off as gently as possible. It hurt, but not unbearably, and at last both feet were free.

'Thank you,' she said, lying back.

He tried to study the damaged foot, frowning. 'It's hard to see while your jeans are covering it.'

'Yes, I really will have to take them off,' she sighed.

'Let me help you. It's all right, I won't look. This is strictly medical.'

'Thanks.'

She opened the buttons at the waist, unzipped the front and began to ease the material down. At first she managed but there came a point when he had to take over. Perdita took a deep breath, raised her hips slightly, balancing on her one good foot, while he drew the jeans towards him, gradually revealing beautiful, slender hips clad in delicate silken panties. But these he didn't see. His head was ostentatiously turned away.

A little further, a bit more—then it was time to pull the jeans over the injured foot.

'Sorry if I hurt you,' he said as she gasped.

'Not your fault.'

'Is anyone staying here with you, anyone I can contact?'

'No.'

'You're alone? There's nobody to look after you?'

'I don't need looking after,' she assured him.

He looked cynical. 'You can lie there and say that, after what's just happened?'

His manner was kind but authoritative, with a touch of 'laying down the law' and she was provoked to say, 'What about you? Is someone looking after you?'

'I don't need looking after,' he echoed her.

'Well, you know the answer to that.'

'Yes, Miss Hanson, I guess I do.'

'How do you know my name?'

'I saw it in your passport when I picked it up off the floor. You are Erica Hanson, and you're English.'

'I guess my passport told you that too.'

'Plus your accent, and the fact that you chose tea.'

'Ah yes, that's a dead giveaway, isn't it?'

A knock on the door announced the arrival of the doctor, a kindly middle-aged man.

'How much does it hurt?' he asked, feeling the ankle.

'Bearable,' Perdita said.

'Good. It's a bit twisted. There's no serious damage but it still needs some rest.'

'You mean I'm going to be confined up here?' she asked, aghast.

'Not necessarily. The hotel can let you have a wheelchair for a day or so. I'll arrange it, plus a walking stick for when you need to leave the wheelchair.'

He bandaged the ankle and gave her some painkillers, then spoke to Leonid. 'I'll come back tomorrow. Can you manage to look after her until then?'

'But—' Perdita began to protest but was silenced by a gesture from Leonid.

'Leave it to me,' he told the doctor.

He saw the man to the door and returned. Perdita was still lying down, now with the duvet modestly pulled up over her hips. It had seemed the right thing to do, although this man had a mysterious quality that didn't make her feel at all modest.

'I can't let you look after me,' she protested.

'You don't have any choice,' he said firmly. 'I've decided.'

'Don't I get a say?'

'Not in the slightest.'

His manner was slightly too hard to be called warm but it wasn't unkind. She guessed he wasn't a patient man, but neither was he entirely unsympathetic. His eyes were dark, shadowed, hinting at fascinating depths full of mysteries. But also hinting at something else, lighter, possibly interesting.

And he was the brother of the man she'd come here to study, she reminded herself. Professional efficiency demanded that she prolong this moment.

'That's kind of you,' she said softly. 'Especially after I gave you so much trouble.'

He made a sound that was half a sigh, half a groan.

'Look, I'd better tell you, I'm not just being nice. There's something in this for me too.'

So the attraction wasn't just on her side, she thought. She held her breath, longing for him to say the next words, and slightly shocked at herself for wanting it so much.

'It's like this,' he said.

But before he could speak there was a knock at the door. He scowled. 'Are you expecting anyone?'

'Nobody,' she said.

He opened the door, revealing an attractive young woman.

'Sorry to barge in,' she said. 'But I've got a message for you, and I saw you carrying a woman upstairs.' She glanced at Perdita, lying in bed. 'I haven't...er...interrupted anything, have I?'

'You have,' he said ironically. 'But not what you're thinking.' He pulled her close for a kiss on the cheek.

Perdita sighed. So that was that.

So much for false hopes.

The young woman was in her twenties, well-dressed and modestly attractive without being a great beauty.

'Where did you vanish to?' she asked Leonid. 'We were all of us about to go to the chapel but suddenly you weren't there.'

'Sorry, Freya, I remembered something I had to do.'

'Are you going to introduce me?' she said, indicating Perdita.

'Freya, this is Erica Hanson. Erica, this is my stepsister. My father is married to her mother.'

'And we bicker like a real brother and sister,' Freya said cheerfully. 'Hello, Erica. It's nice to meet you. Very nice indeed.'

She said the last words with a mysterious significance, and a glance at Leonid that was laden with meaning.

'I'm off to the chapel,' she said. 'They'll be starting the rehearsal soon. Are you coming, Leonid?'

'I'm not sure for the moment—'

'Don't worry, Amos won't be there. He hasn't arrived yet. Anyway, I'll see you later at the family gathering. Erica, I look forward to seeing you there.'

'Well, I don't know if I—'

'Of course you do. Bye for now.'

She hurried out, but not without turning in the doorway and giving them a thumbs up sign.

'What was that all about?' Perdita asked.

'I'm afraid it means that my family is trying to take you over for its own purpose,' he said ruefully. 'Freya has a problem. My father has five sons but no daughter, and he wants to see Freya married off to one of us so that she'll be more than just his stepdaughter. But he's rapidly running out of sons. Darius is already married, Marcel is marrying Cassie tomorrow, and that just leaves three of us.

'We all like Freya but we don't fancy being dictated to. Luckily she doesn't like it either. That's why she was so glad to meet you. She sees you as protection.'

'You mean if your father thinks—?'

'That we're a couple, yes.'

'That will make Freya safe?'

'Safe from me. There's still Jackson and Travis.'

'But isn't Travis—? I mean there's been a lot in the press about his latest love. Surely she'll be here with him?'

'I don't know. Probably, but nobody's really sure about them. We're not even certain that Amos is coming. He's annoyed with Marcel for daring to choose his own wife. But if he does turn up we're all in danger, Jackson, Travis—and me. Unless—' he looked at her with meaning '—unless some guardian angel will be my shield.'

Perdita's lips twitched. 'You mean stand between you and your father and divert his scheming to your brothers?'

'Exactly. I think Freya rather misunderstood the fact that she saw you in bed.'

'But don't you have a girlfriend back wherever you live? From your accent you sound as if you come from a great distance.'

'I live in Moscow.'

'How exciting. And I'm sure you must know a lot of women.'

She had a sense that the question displeased him. His voice was edgy as he replied, 'I have many acquaintances but none that I'm close to in that sense. Otherwise I'd have brought someone with me. Are you attached to anyone?'

'No, I'm a free agent too.'

'So you'll stick with me while we're here, this evening and at the wedding? I'll look after you.' He gave a wry grin and indicated the damp patch on his suit. 'After all, you owe me a favour.'

'Yes, I suppose I do.'

'So you'll be my "shield and protector"?'

She thought no man had ever looked less in need of protection. There was a formidable air about him that contrasted oddly with the flickers of warmth and humour that had begun to appear in his manner.

'Unless you've got other plans,' he added.

'Hardly,' she said, pointing at her foot.

'No, you're going to need me to act as nurse and carer,' he said with a hint of mischievous triumph. 'In fact this suits me so well that you might almost think I caused your fall to suit my own purposes.'

This came uncomfortably near to her own actions, but by now her spirits were rising and she was able to say theatrically, 'Oh, surely not! You could never be so scheming and dishonest.'

He grinned. 'Believe it or not, there are people in the world who'd descend to that.'

'I'm shocked! Shocked!'

'Naturally. You and I rise above such scandalous behaviour.' His eyes gleamed. 'Unless, of course, it's really necessary to push the boundaries.'

'There really are people who sink so low? You must tell me about them.'

'I will. We'll discuss it over dinner tonight. I promise you'll have a good time.'

That depended on how you defined a good time, she thought. So far she was achieving everything she'd wanted—tricking her way into the inner circle, an invitation to the wedding. That wasn't a good time. That was a wonderful, fantastic time.

And as if to underline her good fortune, she had the company of a man whose brooding good looks might have been designed to make everything thrilling. Even his slightly fierce manner, instead of being off-putting, was merely intriguing.

'You don't answer,' he said. 'Are you afraid that I'm going to take advantage? Don't be.' His wolfish eyes gleamed, but his smile softened the look. 'Even if you weren't poorly, this is strictly a performance to convince my father. Just be at my side, and let me put my arm around you so that he can see. But when we're alone you won't have to fight me off, I promise.'

'That makes me feel a lot better,' she said untruthfully.

'Then you'll do it?'

She smiled at him. She had the sudden feeling of standing at the edge of a high cliff. One false step meant danger, but danger didn't frighten her. Danger was like fun: exhilarating.

'I'll do it,' she said.

'Splendid. I'll arrange for the hotel to send you a maid to help you dress, and I'll collect you at six-thirty. And... er...if you'd like to buy a new dress—at my expense—'

'Certainly not!' she said primly. 'I can dress myself appropriately.'

'Of course you can, but—'

'And I *prefer* to dress myself,' she added with a perfectly calculated amount of injured virtue. 'I hope you understand that.'

'Perfectly. Please don't be insulted. I was merely showing my gratitude.'

'But I'm doing this because I want to,' she assured him. 'We agreed that I owe you a favour, since I damaged your suit.'

'Since you—? Oh yes.' He looked down at himself, almost as though remembering for the first time. 'I must go and change. Goodbye. I'll see you later.'

As the door closed behind him she breathed out. He was doing her a much bigger favour than he could imagine, but he mustn't be allowed to suspect. She knew a twinge of guilt, but then determinedly concentrated on the business at hand. Success. That was what really mattered.

The wheelchair arrived an hour later, followed by the maid Leonid had arranged. She assisted Perdita into a dark blue cocktail dress that emphasised her slender figure, while having long sleeves and a high neck. It was just a pity, she thought, that the wheelchair hid most of this. The sooner she was on her feet and able to display her advantages the better.

So much seemed to have happened at the same time. Even through the pain and confusion of her fall she had still been intensely aware of Leonid as a man. She could still feel his arms about her body as he carried her up the stairs, as easily as if she weighed nothing.

The accident restricted her, yet gave her his company as nothing else could have done. It would take time before she knew how she felt about that. But she was smiling at herself in the mirror.

She tried her blonde hair curled high and elaborately, then loose and flowing about her shoulders. Finally she settled for flowing, liking the natural air it gave her.

At precisely six-thirty there was a knock on her door. Leonid was there, handsome in white dinner jacket and bow tie.

'You look almost perfect,' he said seriously.

'Almost?'

'There's just one little thing missing.' He opened a tiny box, revealing a pair of pearl earrings. 'Please accept these and don't be offended. It's just my way of thanking you.'

'I'm not at all offended,' she said truthfully. 'They're so lovely.'

'Let me put them on for you.'

Gently he moved back her hair and fixed the earrings. Perdita watch him in the mirror, trying not to be too conscious of his fingers brushing against her skin.

'Now I must pin my hair up,' she said. 'Otherwise nobody will see them.'

'Does anyone else need to see them?' he asked softly. 'We know they're there.'

'Yes,' she agreed. 'We know.'

He studied her for a moment before letting her hair fall back.

'Beautiful,' he said, taking up his position behind the wheelchair. 'Shall we go?'

As he wheeled her along the corridor she asked, 'Has your father arrived yet?'

'No, but Freya's had a call to say he's on his way.'

Suddenly he paused, looking down the wide staircase, the same one on which she had staged her 'fall'. Below them, in the hall, Perdita could see several young men.

'My brothers,' Leonid said. 'At least, some of them.'

Just then one of the men glanced up, nudged another and pointed.

'That's Darius and his wife, Harriet,' Leonid said. 'Let's make a grand entrance. The elevator's along here.'

As they descended he said, 'By the way, why are you in a wheelchair?'

'What?' she asked, aghast. 'You know why. You were there—'

'I mean what do we tell them?' he explained. 'They're bound to ask about you and we need to say the same thing.'

'Oh yes, of course.'

'If you're going to fool people you have to plan your story in advance,' he said, amused. 'But I guess you're not a very experienced liar, are you?'

'Am I not?' she asked wildly.

'No, otherwise you'd have known that you have to set it up first.'

In fact she knew exactly this. The shock of being mistaken for a naïve newcomer to the art of presentation sent her dizzy.

'I guess I'm just stupid,' she hazarded vaguely.

'No, you're an innocent. You've never learned the art

of scheming. Don't worry, I'm dishonest enough for both of us.'

'Phew! That's a relief. As for the wheelchair, I think we'd better stick to the truth. The hotel people know that I fell downstairs today.'

'You're right,' he said gravely. 'Rely on the truth whenever you can. It saves awkwardness later.'

She glanced up to see how seriously he was speaking, and found him looking down at her with a look of wicked conspiracy that sent a sweet tremor through her.

'Is that experience talking?' she asked.

'What do you think?'

'I think—oh, we're here.'

The doors were opening. And there was his family gazing at the picture they made. Freya must have spread the word about finding them together, but the wheelchair took everyone by surprise. Perdita guessed that none of them would have expected to see Leonid tamely doing such a duty. They all regarded her with friendly curiosity and pressed forward to meet her as he wheeled her out.

'This is Darius, my eldest brother,' Leonid said. 'And this is Marcel, who owns the tatty little shack we're standing in.'

Everyone laughed at this way of describing the luxurious hotel, and Perdita responded, 'I have to say that as tatty little shacks go this is the nicest I've ever seen.'

This brought another laugh. She was becoming a success. She won more approval when she greeted Jackson with admiring remarks about his latest television programme.

A couple had just appeared, hand in hand.

'Travis,' Leonid called. 'Over here.'

The two brothers embraced and made the introductions.

'This is Charlene,' Travis said.

'I've heard a lot about you,' Leonid told her.

'Don't believe all that stuff in the press,' Travis said. 'Nobody knows what she's really like—except me.'

He said this with a warm look that underlined his real meaning. Charlene looked down, blushing slightly.

'And this is Erica,' Leonid told them.

'Whom you've been keeping a big secret,' Travis said.

'We don't all live in the spotlight,' Leonid told him humorously. 'Now, let's go and eat.'

The family were to dine, not in the main restaurant, but in a smaller room nearby that was usually hired for private occasions. Tonight Marcel had commandeered it for himself and his family. Perdita found herself sitting next to him on one side, with Leonid on the other.

Leonid consulted her about the menu. Bearing in mind that they were putting on an act, she gave him all her attention, gazing at his face and responding fervently. When the food was served she faded gracefully into the background so that he could concentrate on his family, thus giving her the chance to study the scene unobserved.

Facing her across the table were Travis and Charlene, who seemed happily absorbed in each other. If their relationship really was a PR con trick they were hiding it splendidly.

'You're doing well,' Leonid said in her ear.

'Thank you. I'm too nervous to say anything very much.'

'Hmm.'

'Hmm?'

'Somehow I can't quite see you as nervous. A woman with your looks never has to worry about her reception. What are you professionally? No, let me guess. A model?'

'What do you think?' she teased.

He looked at her assessingly.

'All right. I think you're undercover, pretending to be an ordinary guest but actually doing something else.'

Her heart nearly stopped. 'Whatever can you mean by that?'

'You're a hotel inspector, checking this place out. Perhaps I ought to warn Marcel about you.'

'Try it. See how you look when he finds out it's not true.'

'All right, I give in. But I'll get it. Just give me a little time and we'll see who wins.'

His smile was charming with a glint of steel, and gave her a faint twinge of guilt at the way she'd wriggled out of the situation. She would never have told him an outright lie, but neither could she tell him the truth at this moment. So avoiding the question was her only option.

I'll tell him later, she promised herself. *Then I can explain, make him understand. But not just yet.*

To her relief, Jackson was indulging in some foolery, enabling her to laugh and divert Leonid's attention.

As the meal drew to a close the diners began to rise and drift out to the balcony overlooking the River Seine. Leonid and Travis stood a little apart, deep in conversation.

'Look at them,' Charlene said at Perdita's elbow. 'So like each other. It comes as a shock to see them together.'

'He told me people often mistake him for Travis, until they get near enough to see the differences,' Perdita said.

'Yes, and those differences aren't really physical. They come from inside. There's a bit of Travis that's a natural clown. He loves laughing at people. He even likes people laughing at him as long as that's what he meant them to do. But Leonid has a dark, gloomy side that's mostly the one he lets people see. At least, that's what Travis has told me. I've only just met him but I can see what Travis means.'

Perdita nodded. Even a brief acquaintance with Leonid was enough for her to have sensed his dark side, and know that it was always there, overshadowing even his brief lighter moments.

'But I dare say you know him better,' Charlene said.

'Some people are easier to know than others,' Perdita hedged. 'I'm sure you've found that out too. As you say, Travis is a laugh a minute, but there must be more to him than that.'

'Oh yes.' Charlene nodded. 'When the press are studying you as closely as they do with him, you have to keep a part of yourself that's just for you and your friends. Hello, what's happened?'

A frisson had gone around the table. Heads turned to regard the tall white-haired man standing at the door.

Amos Falcon, Perdita thought, recognising him from pictures she'd seen in the press. Research had told her far more about him than Leonid realised, how he'd been married several times but seemed incapable of being faithful to any woman.

One by one his sons went to greet him. Darius with an extended hand, Jackson with an embrace, Marcel with a thump on the shoulder. Only Travis and Leonid held back, approaching him slowly and greeting him with restraint.

Perdita saw the way Amos surveyed his sons, and the way they surveyed him. There might be some affection in this family, but there was also a lot of suspicion. She had an instinctive feeling that the young men had inherited enough of their father's nature to be his combatants as well as his sons.

Leonid brought Amos across the room.

'Father, I want you to meet Erica,' he said.

There was the same look of surveillance from Amos, studying her, asking himself if she was a threat to what he wanted.

You bet I'm a threat, she thought. *Because I like getting my own way too.*

Amos brought his wife forward. There were more introductions. Champagne was served. The atmosphere was convivial. Perdita tried to stay modestly in the background, but soon Amos bore down on her.

'It's a pleasure to meet you,' he declared formally. 'Leonid hasn't mentioned you before. How do you come to know each other?'

She drew in a swift breath. She and Leonid had prepared their story as far as the wheelchair was concerned, but they hadn't had time to cover this. Feeling his tension, she thought fast.

'I took a holiday in Moscow,' she said. 'I love the city but I got into a silly muddle, and Leonid rescued me.'

'How did that happen?' Amos asked.

'I really couldn't tell you,' she said, improvising fast. 'I don't speak the language so I didn't understand much of what was happening. I remember I lost my way and took the wrong street but—' She gave Leonid an urgent look.

'It was a lucky chance I happened to be there,' he said quickly. 'After that, I had to keep an eye on her in case she was lost again. And we just…got on well.'

'So when you heard about this wedding you took the chance to see each other?' Amos asked.

Luckily Janine intervened, patting her husband's arm and saying,

'Don't interrogate them, darling. This is a party, not a court case.' She smiled at Perdita. 'See you later.'

She led her husband firmly away.

CHAPTER THREE

LEONID BLEW OUT his breath in relief. 'I blame myself for not being ready for that. Luckily you saved us by your quick thinking.'

'But you're going to have to dream up the story,' she said. 'I know nothing about Moscow.'

'Then weren't you taking a risk setting it there?'

'What else could I do? If I'd said we met in England, or any other part of Europe, your father would have asked when, and whatever I said he might have known that you hadn't been travelling on that date. Moscow was safer because you're there all the time. Oh, goodness!' A terrible thought struck her. 'You are, aren't you?'

'Not quite all the time, but most of it. You're right. Saying Moscow was more convincing.' He turned his head slightly to one side, regarding her with admiration and a hint of suspicion. 'I was wrong about you. You're really good at this.'

She regarded him satirically. 'You mean you don't really think I'm an innocent after all?'

'It means I think there's more than one kind of innocent,' he said, returning her look and speaking carefully.

She burst out laughing. 'Well, you said it.'

'How am I supposed to take that?'

'I couldn't tell you. Only you can decide.'

'Perhaps I should be wary of you.'

'Certainly you should. Behind the mask of innocence I'm just a natural schemer. Don't trust me for a moment. People who know me really well don't even call me Erica.'

'What do they call you?'

'Perdita. It's been my nickname since my father said he'd go to perdition when he heard my mother was pregnant again. It's a family joke that I'm a bit wicked, so Perdita it had to be.'

His eyes gleamed. 'And just how wicked are you?'

She shook her head. 'That's another thing you'll have to learn by experience.'

'Am I a likely victim?'

She appeared to consider this seriously. 'Not really. I don't think you'd be easy to take for a ride.'

'Why's that?'

'Because you're even more cunning and conniving than I am. You as good as told me so yourself.'

'Very astute of you. All right, we've warned each other. Cards on the table.'

'Oh!' she exclaimed. 'On the table? You mean you won't even keep one little ace up your sleeve? How disappointing!'

'I take that as a warning that you'll keep a concealed ace yourself.'

'Naturally. Without aces, the world would be no fun.'

'Fun?' For a moment he looked puzzled, as though he'd never heard the word before.

'You do know what fun is, don't you?' she challenged him.

'I think I heard of it once, somewhere,' he said, playing up to her.

'But you don't know how desperately important it can

be. How it can light up life so that you have something to hold onto in the dark times.'

'There are many things I've never discovered,' Leonid said seriously. 'Who knows? Perhaps I shall learn them from Perdita. Or do I mean Erica?'

'They come and they go,' she said lightly. 'Sometimes even I can't keep track. But it makes life interesting.'

'Yes, I should imagine that life with you is very interesting.'

She was about to give him a teasing answer when something caught her attention.

'Look,' she said.

'What?'

'Over there. The way your father is staring at us.'

'He's suspicious. He thinks this is a con. I guess our performance didn't fool him.' He smiled at her. 'We'll have to do better.'

'How dare he suspect us of deception!' she said with comic indignation. 'That's insulting.'

He laughed. 'Of course. How could anyone think we'd stoop so low?'

'Go on laughing,' she said quickly. 'It looks convincing.'

Far too convincing, warned her inner voice. Despite the fact that one side of him was grim and nearly ferocious, or perhaps because of it, Leonid's smile had an intensity that was almost shocking.

'Look into my eyes,' he murmured, 'and try to forgive me for what I'm about to do.'

Sighing theatrically, she aimed a yearning glance up at his face. He took her hand, raising it gently to his mouth and brushing his lips against the back. Then, as if acting on a sudden impulse, he turned it over and buried his mouth in her palm, sending heated impulses along her nerves, so that she had to struggle not to gasp.

'Sorry,' he murmured, returning her hand, though he didn't sound sorry at all.

'No need to be sorry,' she whispered back, meaning it.

Lucky I'm not naïve, she thought. *Or I could get carried away.*

'How long are you here for?' he asked, straightening up and trying to appear normal again.

'I'm…not sure.'

'You don't have to be home by a certain date?'

'I choose the date,' she said lightly. 'I like to keep my choices open.'

'So you're free to take a holiday whenever you choose? Don't tell me, let me guess. You've got a rich indulgent father who sends you anywhere you want.'

'Do I look like a spoiled brat?' she demanded with mock indignation. 'I can afford to pay my own bills, thank you.'

'In this place?' he said, looking around at the luxurious surroundings.

'In any place,' she assured him.

He gave a knowing glance at her expensive clothes.

'You certainly know how to dress for effect. I think—'

Suddenly his smile died. He was looking at the far side of the room, where Janine was absorbed in a conversation with Marcel. Amos was now standing alone.

'Excuse me a moment,' he said. 'I need to have a private word with my father. I'll be back.'

'Don't worry, I can manage alone.'

He hurried over and drew Amos aside, speaking in a low, urgent voice. 'We need to talk, Father. It's important. I'm glad you managed to get here.'

'Frankly, I don't think this marriage is a good idea, but Marcel won't listen to me.'

'He's in love with Cassie,' Leonid reminded him. 'Doesn't that make it a good idea? I'm sure you can appreciate love. You've enjoyed it often enough.'

'Yes, well, never mind that. How is your mother? In the best of health, I trust?'

'She hasn't been in the best of health for a long time, as I'm sure I've told you before.'

'Sorry to hear that. But she's not a young woman. We're none of us as young as we were.'

'That's very true. And it's why I hope to persuade you to pay us a visit. It would mean the world to her to see you again.'

'Or it might upset her. I wouldn't want to do that.'

'Wait until you see her letter that I've brought you.'

'Not now. Tomorrow will do.'

'I'll deliver it to your room later tonight, so you'll have time to write your reply and give it to me tomorrow.'

'No need for that. I can put it in the post.'

'I promised her I'd take it back with me. She's very lonely, Father. I'd rather keep my word.'

'Very well. Arrange things however you wish, but tomorrow. Not tonight.'

Watching from the far side of the room, Perdita couldn't hear the words, but she had a clear view of Leonid's face. At the start he'd appeared fairly amiable, yet she had a sense of tension held in check, as though he could never truly relax with his father. Then she saw his manner change, his lips tighten, his eyes grow darker. As the two men turned away from each other she saw in his face something that boded ill for anyone who crossed him.

Then he caught her looking at him. His expression cleared and his smile returned.

That was only part of their performance, she told herself. But as he neared her she could have sworn she saw warmth again in his eyes.

Marcel and Cassie came close.

'We're having an early night,' he said. 'It's a busy day tomorrow.'

'Good idea!' Travis said.

Soon everyone was drifting away towards the elevators. Upstairs they headed for the corridor where they were all staying. Leonid wheeled Perdita towards her room and, mindful of Amos's watchful eye, leaned down so that his head was on a level with hers.

'We're nearly at your door,' he murmured. 'They're looking to see if I come inside with you. We mustn't disappoint them.'

'Mustn't we? Perhaps I have something to say about that.' She gave a gasp of theatrical horror. 'What kind of girl do you think I am? The kind who invites a man to her room just because he showed her around Moscow?'

He grinned. 'I guess I've been meeting the wrong kind of girls.'

'I'm sure you have,' she teased. 'And I'll bet you've enjoyed every minute of it.'

'Are you suggesting that I'm a man who plays around with every female he can lay his hands on?'

'Are you suggesting that you're not?'

Their eyes met in perfect amused understanding.

'I'll answer that tomorrow,' he murmured. 'Right now I think any answer I gave would be the wrong one.'

'Probably. Some men have an infallible gift for getting it wrong.'

His voice dropped to a low whisper. 'I could make you pay for that.'

'You could try.'

'Think I can't?'

She chuckled softly. 'Surely you wouldn't take revenge on a poor frail creature in a wheelchair?'

'Certainly not. I promised to take care of you, so now I'm coming in to undress you and put you to bed.'

Her eyes gleamed in appreciation of these tactics. This was an experienced foe, up to every trick, and challenging him was fun.

'Very kind,' she said. 'But I haven't asked you to do that.'

'A gentleman doesn't wait for a lady to request his help. He volunteers his services.'

'And if she says she doesn't require them?'

He looked surprised. 'Did I ask your opinion?'

'No, I can't imagine you asking anyone else what they thought.'

'I'm glad you understand me so well. Now, we're nearly there, and they're all finding excuses to linger in the corridor and observe us.'

'So they'll see you come in.'

'More than that. I'm going to kiss you. And no power on earth can stop me.'

'Then I won't waste time trying,' she assured him.

This time his hand was on her shoulder. As he lowered his head she almost thought he would indulge in a passionate embrace, but he was too clever for that. In full view of his family he drew her close for a brief touch of the lips, lingering just long enough for a soft caress, then drawing modestly back.

As he wheeled her inside she caught a last glimpse of the family observing them, and knew by their expressions that Leonid had been right.

'Your father's really cross with you,' she said.

'Good. That's the idea.'

Yes, that was what this was really all about, she thought. Leonid was doing this to gain something for himself, and a sensible woman wouldn't let herself forget that.

But was she a sensible woman?

She'd been sensible enough when she'd arrived here, thinking only of professional success, sure that she was armoured against anything else that could happen.

Which just showed how little she knew. Life was more complicated than she'd thought, and she was struggling to catch up.

Leonid seemed untroubled by such thoughts. He was getting to work, kneeling down before her to remove her shoes.

'Now lean forward,' he said.

She did so and he began to undo the buttons at the back of the dress.

'Where's your nightie?'

She pointed to a drawer. 'Over there.'

He fetched it and tossed it onto the bed. 'Now stand. Mind your foot.'

Clutching him, she managed to get up, wondering how far he intended to take this. He drew up her dress, pulling it over her head.

'I guess you can manage from here,' he said.

'Yes, I can sit down on the bed to deal with everything else. Thank you.'

He took out a small card and scribbled something on the back.

'That's my room number. Call me if you need help. Any time.'

'I'm sure I'll be all right.'

'Give me your word.'

'All right. I promise.'

'I'm just down the corridor if you need me. Don't forget.'

'I won't,' she said gratefully.

He opened the door gingerly and looked out into the corridor. After a moment he looked back at her, nodded and left.

When he'd gone the silence seemed to thunder. Perdita sat taking deep breaths, trying to come to terms with the altered universe in which she was living.

Slowly she removed her underwear. He hadn't touched those intimate garments, and all her senses told her why. He feared to go further, feared to see her naked. Yet she could have sworn that it had nearly happened.

Some deep, primitive instinct told her that Leonid had been on the verge of losing control, kissing her with passion, locking the door and saying to hell with the rest of the world.

That would have been alarming.

But not nearly as alarming as the intensity with which she'd wanted it to happen.

The corridor was empty, the Falcon family having drifted away when they'd seen what they were curious to see.

Now Leonid stood there alone, motionless. Even knowing of her injury, he couldn't help indulging a wild fantasy in which she hobbled to the door and pulled it open to summon him back. So many women had closed doors to him, only to open them with a beckoning finger a moment later.

At last he talked sense to himself and moved away quietly to his own room. He had come to Paris prepared for the unexpected, as he always did with family meetings, but this time events had conspired to knock him sideways. It was like being slammed back against a wall, with no idea what to do about it.

He was a man who valued being in control above all else. Suddenly he had no control left. That was disquieting, but it roused another aspect of himself, one he'd barely known existed. Sooner or later he must regain control, but first he would wait and learn more.

He looked at himself in the mirror, half expecting not to recognise the man he saw there.

He'd been staggered by how he'd felt carrying her upstairs. She wasn't the first woman he'd lifted in his arms. Far from it. But the others had always been expensive ladies, their bodies pressed voluptuously against his because they knew where he was taking them and why; knew what they would give and what he would give, because the bargain was sealed in advance. That was how he liked it.

But this girl's body wasn't voluptuous, only frail. There could be no bargain, only the awareness of her helpless need, demanding that he give and give; and his own unexpected willingness to do exactly that.

But what warmed his heart more than anything was the fact that this meeting hadn't been planned in advance. Unlike his encounters with various expensive women, this one had been unplanned, spontaneous, and the more beautiful for that. It was as though Fate had tapped him on the shoulder and whispered, *I'm still here, you know. From now on, I'll make the arrangements.*

He smiled.

As she finished dressing next morning, Perdita's cellphone rang.

'Hi, it's Gary. I thought you'd have called me before this.'

Gary was the editor of a glitzy magazine specialising in 'hot' celebrity stories. He was her best customer, but just now he was the last person she wanted to talk to.

'How are you doing?' he asked jovially. 'C'mon, I'm dying to hear about your latest scoop. Don't tell me you haven't got close to the family—'

'Well—'

She was standing by the window, looking down into the street below. There was Leonid, standing by the River Seine, looking out over the water. Glancing up, he saw her and smiled.

'I'm sorry, Gary. There's nothing yet.'

'Nothing? Usually you've got it all sorted long before this.'

'I guess I'm just not being as tricksy as usual,' she said thoughtfully.

'No kidding! What's gone wrong?'

'Nothing's gone wrong. Everything's fine.'

She hung up quickly and stared at the phone, wondering at herself.

Despite her denial, something really had gone wrong. Suddenly she wasn't her usual self, playing one angle against another, caring for nothing except what she wanted.

She was making a success of this job, accepted into the inner circle, invited to the wedding, trusted by Leonid.

And there lay the problem. Leonid trusted her. And that trust was sacred.

Was it a malign or a generous fate that had shown him her passport with the name Erica Hanson, so that he knew nothing of Perdita Davis, the journalist?

Now the warmth in his eyes seemed to haunt her. This was a man who didn't give his trust or his warmth easily. But he'd given it to her. And no power on earth would make her betray him.

I'm going crazy, she thought. *After today I'll never see him again, so why shouldn't I—? Why? Why?*

From the corridor outside came a sudden noise. Two men were arguing. One of them was Leonid.

'I said get the hell out of here and I meant it. Just go now, and don't let me see you here again, pestering my family.'

'Look, I only—' the other man protested.

Instantly Perdita froze. She knew that voice. It belonged to Frank, the photojournalist she'd known briefly a few years ago.

'I said get out.' Leonid's voice was full of rage.

There came the sound of footsteps racing along the corridor, then a knock at her door.

She was full of fear. Had Frank really gone? He mustn't find her here, because he could tell Leonid things about her that she wasn't ready for him to know.

She managed to limp to the door and open it, while standing back, so as not to be seen from the corridor. But only Leonid was there.

'Was that a fight I heard?' she asked.

'I've just had a bitter encounter with a man who's been sneaking around trying to invade this wedding. He's got a camera, so I guess he's a journalist pursuing Travis.'

'Travis must be used to that,' she said.

'Normally, yes, but this wedding is Marcel's and it's private. And Travis may not be the only prey. They chase my father too, trying to find something scandalous. Damn all journalists, deceitful, devious monsters!'

He strode over to the window to look down into the street.

'There he is, leaving, thank goodness! Come and look.'

'No, I must—'

Quickly she vanished into the bathroom. She shuddered as she thought what might have happened if she'd gone to the window. Frank could have looked up and recognised her, and that would have been a disaster.

Devious, deceitful. They were the kindest things Leonid would have called her. And that mustn't happen. She didn't know where the road led, but she knew that she wanted no distractions.

As she emerged from the bathroom Leonid turned away from the window.

'Time to go down to breakfast,' he said. 'Then to the chapel for the wedding.'

'Are you sure you want to take me?' she was impelled to say. 'It's such a private thing—they've gone to so much trouble to keep strangers out—'

He looked determined. 'But you're not a stranger. I wouldn't have invited you if I didn't know I could trust you.'

Perdita wished he hadn't said that. She was barely able to speak for the storm of emotion that invaded her, but she just managed to thank him.

She knew now that there would be no story.

As they left the room she noticed a slip of white paper just appearing at the top of his pocket. Seeing her look, he pushed it further down.

'It's a letter from my mother to my father. I promised her I'd give it to him but I can't seem to get him alone. And I don't want to upset Janine by doing it while she's there.'

'Leave it to me,' she said.

'No, I can't ask you to give it to him.'

'That's not what I meant. Just wait, and be ready to pounce when the moment comes.'

His look of total bafflement gave her one of the most enjoyable moments she'd ever known.

Today she had abandoned the wheelchair and managed

to limp slowly and carefully into the elevator, clinging to Leonid's arm.

'Are you all right?' he asked anxiously.

'I'm just fine.'

They entered the breakfast room to find the older couple already seated. Perdita plonked herself down beside Janine, laughing, admiring her dress, making merry chatter. Out of the corner of her eye she saw Leonid approach Amos. For a few minutes she occupied Janine's total attention, only stopping when she saw Amos take the letter from his son and thrust it into an inner pocket. Then she moved away to where the food was laid out, and waited until Leonid joined her.

'Mission accomplished?' she murmured.

'Definitely. And thank you. You're a genius.'

'No, I'm not,' she teased. 'I'm just a silly gossipy female who can't shut up for five minutes.'

'At this moment that looks like just another way of saying genius.'

Breakfast was a hurried meal. Amos glared at everyone, which didn't seem to trouble them. Evidently they were used to it, Perdita thought.

Then it was time for the wedding. Marcel took his place, with Darius as his best man. The bride was approaching. As Marcel turned to look at her with adoration in his eyes Perdita saw Travis and Charlene put their heads together, absorbed in some private world.

They're really in love, she thought. *What a story. What a scoop! If only I could use it.*

Perhaps another time, she thought wistfully. Just now other things were more important.

The wedding reception was a triumph that would have sent her into journalistic heaven had things been different. But she'd resolved to make a sacrifice for Leonid's sake, and she was a woman of her word.

Limping carefully about the room, sipping champagne, she came to the family group. Leonid was mourning the fact that soon they would say goodbye, go their separate ways and not know when next they would meet.

'But that's easy,' Charlene said. 'Travis's TV show filmed an episode in London, so why not an episode in Moscow?'

Leonid thumped Travis on the shoulder, saying, 'Just wait until you get to Moscow and I can boast that this is my brother. Travis, your lady is a genius.'

'Come on, I only suggested it,' Charlene laughed. 'If they do this it will be to please Travis.'

'True,' Leonid agreed. 'Travis is the great man. But a great man needs a great lady beside him all the time.'

'He certainly does,' Travis said, glancing at Charlene, but then glancing quickly at Perdita as if to say that Leonid had his own great lady.

Leonid followed his gaze with a look in his eyes that Perdita wished she understood.

The trill of a cellphone made Travis say, 'Damn! Why does the phone have to ring now? Hello, Joe!—What's that?' Then his face brightened. 'Are you sure? It's not a mistake?'

What is it?' Charlene asked.

'It's the nominations for the TopGo Television Awards. The firm's had some advance notice.'

'And you've got a nomination?' Darius demanded.

It turned out that he had four nominations. Everybody cheered and made a note of the date, the following month.

'So we'll all meet again,' Travis said, looking around.

'Definitely,' Leonid agreed. 'Nothing would make me miss this.'

'Nor I,' Amos said unexpectedly. 'My boy, you've done us credit.'

Janine was watching everything with a pleased smile. She moved closer to Perdita until she could murmur in her ear, 'I'm really grateful to you for deflecting Amos's fire.'

'I don't know what you mean,' Perdita said carefully.

'Very shrewdly answered, but I think you do know. I'd never want to see Freya married to Leonid. He's a real grim character.'

'You don't know that,' Perdita said. 'How often have you met him?'

'Only once before, this but that was enough. Like I say, I'm grateful to you, but don't make the mistake of getting too involved with him. He'd make you regret it.'

'I'll bear your warning in mind,' she said, withdrawing before her indignation overcame her. She could understand why Janine saw Leonid in this way, but it was a shallow judgement, and part of her wanted to leap to his defence. In the brief time she'd known him she sensed that there was a great deal more to him than 'hard as nails'.

But why should she brood about that? she wondered sadly. In a few hours they would say goodbye. He would return to Russia and she to England. Would they ever see each other again? Almost certainly not.

She shivered.

CHAPTER FOUR

At last Leonid managed to draw Amos aside and say quietly, 'Father have you read Mother's letter?'

'Yes, I've read it.'

'Then you have a reply for me to take home?'

'Not yet. Give me a little time—'

'But you're leaving early tomorrow. Surely—'

'Stop hassling me,' Amos growled. Abruptly his manner changed and he raised his voice. 'Ah, Marcel, there you are. Let me embrace the groom.'

He slid away, leaving Leonid seething.

'Are you all right?' Perdita asked, approaching from a distance, where she'd been watching them.

'No, I'm far from all right,' he growled. 'I need to get out into the garden. Let me see you upstairs first.'

'No, I'd like to come with you—that is, if I may.'

She didn't say it but he looked like a man who shouldn't be alone. Whatever could his father have said to put him in this mood?

'I'm in a vile temper,' he said. 'I'll probably vent it on you.'

'I've been warned. Come on, let's go. Take my arm and walk carefully.'

Outside the hotel was a large garden, stretching along the Seine. Dusk was falling and the river was brilliant with lights from boats from which music floated. They found a quiet spot where they could be alone.

'What's gone wrong?' she asked when they were settled.

'Nothing that I shouldn't have expected,' he said with a frustrated growl.

'Your father?'

'Yes. I spoke to him about my mother's letter, asked him about the reply he's supposed to be sending her. Damn him!'

'You obviously don't get on well with him.'

'I'm like all his other sons. We get on well when I do what he wishes. If I don't he prefers not to know me. He's great at business, and he wants us to be the same. He judges us by how close we come to his standard.'

'But you're a successful businessman, aren't you? Doesn't he see you as a chip off the old block?'

'Mostly, yes. We've done some deals together in the past, and I try to keep on his right side. Not for my own sake but for my mother's. She fell in love with him a long time ago, and she's never got over him, although it's years since they last met.'

He became silent, lowering his head, and Perdita saw how his shoulders had sagged. Moved by a surge of sympathy, she reached out and let her arm slide around his neck. She half expected him to flinch away, but he didn't. Instead he moved closer until his head was almost touching hers.

'She married very young,' he said. 'Her parents chose the man for her and I don't think she had much say. His name was Dmitri Tsarev. She wasn't happy. People who knew them then have told me that he wanted a son, but she couldn't seem to get pregnant. Then she met Amos, who'd come to Russia to explore business possibilities. They met in a country house in the south, near the Don River. Her parents owned it and she was visiting them while Amos was in the neighbourhood, and fell in love with him.

'But he…well, I think he just enjoyed himself, as with so many other women, then went home and forgot her. He was married to Marcel's mother at the time. But when he'd gone she found herself pregnant. She tried to contact him but it was a long time before she managed it. In the meantime I'd been born and Dmitri was thrilled to think he had a son.

'In many ways he was a good father to me in those early years. He loved me and treated me well, but only because he thought I was his. Then Amos returned to Russia and everything was revealed. Dmitri threw us both out. My mother thought Amos would take us both back to England with him, but he didn't. He gave her money but left us behind.

'She's never got over that. After all these years she lives in a world where Amos truly loves her and would be with her if he could. I live in Moscow and would like to have her with me, but she's still in her parents' house, which she inherited. It's where they were together, and she won't leave it.'

'Did her husband never soften towards her?'

'No. He died a few years ago, still without softening to either of us, but I don't think she felt that very much. It's Amos's desertion that broke her heart. She's never really let herself believe it. She's sure that one day he'll come to her. I used to try to make her see the truth, but I gave that up. She couldn't bear it. So I've given him her letter and I'll make him reply, although it'll be a struggle. She wants me to take him back to visit her, but I know he won't come, and she'll be left again in the dismal limbo that I can't do anything about.'

He slammed a fist down on his knee, then again and again. His whole attitude was redolent of anger, despair and misery.

'I can't—do anything—about it—' he raged. 'She depends on me and I let her down every time.'

'Leonid, don't talk like that,' Perdita said fiercely. 'It's not your fault. You weren't to blame for your mother's misfortune.'

'But I'm all she has,' he groaned. 'She loved him totally, giving everything she was, and he left her with nothing.'

'No, he didn't. He left her a son to love, which means she hasn't lost everything.'

'But what use am I? I can't console her grief. I can't make up for her losing him.'

'While you're there she hasn't lost him. Not completely. Part of him remains in her life, loving her, thinking of her, concerned for her. As long as she has you, Amos Falcon is still part of her life.'

He grew very still. Then he raised his head and studied her face, frowning with concentration as he struggled to accept what she guessed was a strange point of view to him.

'She may not have very much happiness in her life,' Perdita added, 'but what little she has comes from you, and only you.'

'I suppose…that's true,' he said softly. 'I never thought of it like that.'

'Well, you should. She's a lucky woman because she has a son who loves her and worries about her.'

'But it torments me that I can't really help her. I want her to be happy. I want to make him treat her properly, but—' He made a helpless gesture. 'What can I do? *What can I do?*'

'There's always his letter to her. That could say things that will make her happy.'

'If I can get him to write it. Why won't he even take that little bit of trouble?'

'Probably because he can't think what to say,' Perdita mused. 'From what little I've seen of him, I don't think he's a man to whom emotions come easily.'

'I sometimes think they don't come at all,' Leonid growled. 'Except when it suits him.'

'Then you must help him, for your mother's sake.'

'What makes you think he'd let me tell him what to write?' Leonid asked, carefully.

'He might actually prefer you to tell him, because it would save him having to work it out himself.'

Leonid's eyes were fixed on her with a look of wonder, like a man seeing a magic spell come to life.

'Yes, of course he would,' he murmured.

'Tell him to say that he's always thinking of her, especially when he sees you. The two of you can talk about her and that brings him happiness.'

'Wait,' Leonid said urgently, reaching into his pocket for a small notebook and pencil. 'Go on.'

'He should say how proud he is of you and what it means to him to see how well she's raised his son. Do you look at all like her?'

'I believe I've got her eyes, so they tell me.'

'Good. He likes your eyes because they remind him of her. And what about the place where she lives? Didn't you say that was where they met?'

'Yes, Rostov. It's by the Don River. They used to stroll by the water in the evening.'

'Then it means a lot to him to know that she's still there. He remembers the river and pictures her walking there, thinking about him. Has he ever told you anything he specially recalls about those walks?'

He screwed up his eyes in a desperate attempt to re-call something.

'I don't think—no, but she has. I remember now. While he was there they visited Taganrog, another town nearby. She showed it to him and talked about the famous peo-ple who'd once lived there, or visited—Tchaikovsky and Chekhov. Later he told her that he'd barely heard her. He was just thinking how beautiful her eyes were.'

'Has he ever mentioned that in any letter to her?'

'Never. I don't think he remembers any of it. She told me. But he's going to remember now. I'll get him to put this in his own handwriting, and she'll be so happy. Thank you. *Thank you!'*

Before she knew what he meant to do he'd seized her shoulders and planted a fierce kiss on her mouth.

'I'm sorry,' he said hurriedly, 'I shouldn't have done that—after what you've done for me—to force myself on you—'

'Don't worry. I forgive you,' she said lightly. 'Now hurry back inside so that you can corner your father. Don't wait for me. I can manage if I walk slowly.'

'Are you sure?'

'Get going. I'll see you later.'

He turned and fled. She watched him vanish into the dusk, glad that he hadn't lingered long enough to sense the way her heart had started to thunder as he kissed her. Despite its power, it had been a kiss of gratitude. And she didn't wanted him to know how it had affected her.

Not yet anyway.

Voices seemed to clamour in her mind. Hortense called Leonid 'hard as nails'. Janine had called him a 'grim char-acter', which was unfair, given the concern for her feelings that he'd shown by not handing over the letter in her presence.

Neither of you know him, Perdita thought. *He's not hard. He's so vulnerable that he scares himself. That grim face is like a metal visor.*

She eased her way back to the hotel and slipped in quietly, careful not to be noticed by those of the family who were still celebrating. In the corridor upstairs she paused by Amos's room. From inside, she could just hear his voice and tensed, listening and hoping to hear another voice.

Then it came. Leonid was there with his father, making use of the tool she'd given him to achieve his heart's desire. His voice grew closer, as though he was approaching the door, and she moved fast, hurrying to her own room. He must not find her here.

Once there she poured herself a glass of wine, knowing that the next hour would be the most difficult she had ever known.

At last came the knock on her door. Opening it, she saw a man with the most gentle face she had ever seen. She took his hand and drew him inside, certain that now he would take her in his arms. But he only stood looking down at her with an expression that was strangely confused.

'What I owe you cannot be put into words,' he said softly.

'Did it go well?'

'Well?' he echoed in wonder. 'You have given me such a gift that no thanks will ever be enough. You were right about my father. He needed someone to tell him what to say, and with your help he wrote a letter that will make my mother happy.'

'Your help, not mine,' she suggested.

'No, I could never have done it alone. But I must admit

that when he said he was glad of my suggestions, I didn't tell him about you. I should have done but I'm afraid I took all the credit.'

'Good!' she said urgently. 'If you'd mentioned me it would have spoiled everything. You must never tell him.'

'If I don't—isn't that a little dishonest?'

'Yes, and you should make the most of it. Too much honesty can be a big mistake. Sometimes the best and kindest thing is to let people believe what they want to believe, whether it's true or not. But you do that all the time with your mother.'

He nodded slowly. 'I'll do whatever you say.'

She smiled at him, full of tenderness. 'Don't let your employees hear you say a thing like that. Your reputation would never recover.'

He nodded. 'They wouldn't understand, because they don't know you; how kind and sweet you are.' He pulled out an envelope. 'Without you, this could never have been written. Would you like to read it?'

'No,' she said quickly, backing away. 'That's private. I have no right to read it.'

'How can you say that after the way you inspired it?'

'Leonid, that's *his* letter to her.' She took his face between her hands and spoke urgently. 'Nobody else had anything to do with it. You must keep telling yourself that. Whatever he said, she'll long to believe it came from him. You must never, never let her think otherwise.'

'You're right,' he said slowly.

'It would ruin it for her if she ever suspected the truth.'

'Then I can't even tell her that you were so kind and helpful?'

'She doesn't want my kindness. She wants his kindness. Besides, she doesn't know me. I'd just be a meaningless name to her. Tomorrow we'll each go our own way, and she need never hear of me.'

'Each go our own way,' he echoed slowly. 'You speak as though we'll never see each other again.'

'Perhaps we won't. I live in London and you in Moscow.'

'But we *must* meet again. Next month is the awards ceremony in Los Angeles. I shall be there, and you—?'

'Yes, I shall be there.'

'We'll have time to talk and…and see what happens.'

'Yes,' she whispered. 'Yes.'

He reached out and drew her towards him as gently as if he feared she would break. His lips touched hers lightly, and she waited for his grip to tighten, his embrace to become passionate. Now she knew that this was what she wanted with all her heart. Nothing else mattered but to be in his arms, feeling his passion rise to meet her own.

But then he became still and drew back from her, breathing hard. She could feel him trembling. Or perhaps it was her own trembling she could feel. She couldn't be sure.

'Darling,' he said in a shaking voice. 'You know what I want?'

Her heart leapt. 'Yes, I know.'

'But you have given me so much. I won't…I can't ask for more. At least not tonight—'

'You don't have to ask,' she whispered. 'Neither of us has to ask anything from the other. Leonid, what's troubling you?'

'I want you too much.'

'Can there be too much?'

He released her, taking a step back.

'Yes, if we…if I…no, I don't mean that. You couldn't understand, because even I don't understand…about you… about me—about everything. I can't do this. *I can't.*'

The next moment the door had slammed and she was alone, hearing his footsteps vanish down the corridor as though he couldn't get far enough away from her.

It was a strange night that followed. Perdita spent it sitting by the window, wondering at the contradictory feelings that stormed through her.

Both her emotions and her body had reached out to Leonid, wanting him completely. And he'd backed away, escaping her as fast as he could.

Logically, I should feel horribly rejected, she mused.

But then a soft smile came over her face.

To hell with logic. Logic can take a running jump.

Every instinct told her that Leonid wanted her as much as she wanted him; wanted her more than his super-controlled nature could cope with. It wasn't her he'd fled, but himself.

But I won't let you go. We'll have a little time tomorrow before we say goodbye, and next month we'll meet again in Los Angeles.

Or perhaps he would return tonight.

One thing was sure. The time had come when she must tell him the truth. Tomorrow, before they parted, she would admit that she'd come here with a secret purpose, but it hadn't lasted. Their meeting had changed everything, and she'd abandoned that purpose.

Perhaps he would doubt her honesty at first, but her heart told her that in the end all would be well. The mysterious feeling that had grown between them was powerful enough to fight the problems.

And then? she wondered. What did the future hold?

Down below was the River Seine, dark and mysterious or glittering with lights. The lights would fade, she thought, looking down, but the mystery would always be there. She could see the tall figure of a man. He was too far away for her to see who he was, but she felt that she knew.

Sometimes he glanced up at her window. Suppose she leaned out and waved to him? Would he come up to her?

But then he turned aside and hurried away into the night. And she knew that he wouldn't come to her tonight.

The knock on her door came next morning just as she finished dressing. By now she could manage to walk more easily.

'You're getting there,' he said, delighted.

'Yes, I'm much better.'

'About last night—I'm sorry. You must think I'm mad. It's what I think about myself.'

She shook her head, feeling again the tender protectiveness that he could inspire in her so easily.

'No, I don't. Things converged on us and we didn't have time to know how we felt.'

He nodded eagerly. 'I knew you'd understand, because you understand everything. Look, do you have to return to England today?'

'No, I have some free time.'

'So have I, just one day. I can postpone my flight until tomorrow, and we could spend today here together. The others will be gone and we can be alone.'

She nodded, thrilled. There was nothing she wanted more.

'Yes,' she whispered.

'Yes,' he agreed, drawing her close.

She was ready for his kiss, eager for it, reaching for him as he did for her. Every touch, every caress told her the strength of his desire, equal to her own. They would spend today together as he had said, getting to know each other in every way. And then—?

A sharp ringing filled the room.

'Damn!' he groaned, reaching into his pocket for a cell-phone. 'I'll get rid of them quickly.'

But she knew that wouldn't happen as soon as she saw the change in his face and heard the edgy note in his voice as he exclaimed, *'Nina!'*

After that he spoke Russian. She didn't understand the words but she knew their beautiful day was over before it had begun. Leonid was asking questions in a voice full of anxiety. Once he paused briefly to say to her, 'Nina looks after my mother. She seems to be in a bad way. *Mamma!'*

Again she couldn't follow the words, but she didn't need to. The tone of his voice told her everything. Now he was speaking to someone that he loved tenderly, offering her kindness and reassurance through the note in his voice. No need for words. When he hung up Perdita was sadly certain what he was going to say.

'I have to hurry back,' he said. 'It seems my mother misunderstood the day I was supposed to be going home to her. She thought it would be today and she's deeply distressed. Nina has tried to comfort her, but without success.'

'Then you must get home quickly,' Perdita said. 'She needs you.'

'I'm so sorry.'

'You have nothing to be sorry about. You owe me nothing and her everything.'

'Bless you for that. Bless you for your sweet understanding. But we'll see each other again next month.'

'Of course we will.'

'I don't know how I'll endure the wait. You will be there, won't you? You must say yes, because if you don't I'll come and fetch you.'

'You don't have to give me orders,' she told him, amused.

'Sorry, sorry—it's just that I—'

It was just that he was used to laying down the law, she thought; except to the sad woman on the end of the phone.

'It's all right,' she reassured him. 'I'll be there.'

The change in his face was astonishing, and moving. One moment he was 'the master', insisting on his way and no other. Next moment he was a grateful supplicant, full of touching relief.

'You won't be sorry, I promise you,' he said. 'We'll have a wonderful time together, and perhaps this time you'll let me buy you a present—'

'I have the pearls.'

'I mean a proper present.'

'You don't need to. I'm not out to make a profit from you.'

'I know that. If only I could...well, we'll talk and really get to know each other.'

'That's what I want too.'

'Now I must dash to the airport. I would give anything for this not to have happened. I wanted to be with you so much today but—you understand—I must do what I can for her.'

'Our time will come,' she promised.

Even through the depths of her disappointment she loved him for his kindness to the pathetic woman who depended on him.

They travelled to the airport together, and clasped each other in a final fond embrace. Throughout the flight home Perdita sat in a happy daze. A new road was opening ahead of her, and though it was too soon to say for certain where it led, her heart told her that happiness lay in wait. It was illogical, unreasonable, irrational. But these things had never troubled her before. And she wasn't going to let them trouble her now.

CHAPTER FIVE

ALL THE WAY home Leonid had dreaded the meeting with his mother. He knew how her eyes would brighten with hope at the first sight of him, then darken again when she saw he was alone. Worse still was his confusion about the letter. Should he give it to her? It would surely be wisest not to.

His mother was waiting in the garden, looking eagerly hopeful then sad, just as he'd feared. He embraced her vigorously, doing everything in his power to cheer her up, longing for some miracle to give her the happiness that he couldn't.

'I'm sorry, Mamma,' he said when they were seated. 'Father had to dash off to an important meeting, otherwise he'd have loved to see you again.'

'Yes, I suppose there was bound to be something. He's such a busy and important man. It's strange when you consider how old he is, and how much more time he must have these days than in the past.'

'Men like Father don't really retire,' he said. 'There's always some business to absorb them.'

Secretly he knew she was right. What business arrangements Amos had these days weren't enough to stop him doing anything he wanted. But, as always, he reassured her with a gentle fiction.

Too much honesty can be a big mistake.

The voice, whispering in his mind, made him tense and look around him uneasily.

'What is it, my dear?' Varushka asked.

'Nothing, Mamma.'

'You jumped as if something had startled you.'

'No—everything's all right.'

'Did Amos send me a letter?'

He'd wrestled with himself, thinking it might be better not to give it to her. But now he knew that he had no choice.

He watched her face as she read it, saw her gasp and cover her mouth as the tears started.

'Mamma—'

'He remembered—after all this time he still remembers.'

'What is it?'

'The time we met, when we went walking through the streets of Taganrog.' She began to read. '"You told me about the town, and the famous people who'd been there, but I only half listened. I was watching you, entranced by how beautiful you were, how gentle your voice. At last I told you that, but I don't think you believed me. You should have done. How could I be interested in Tchaikovsky and Chekhov when I was with you?"'

She laid down the letter. 'I thought he must have forgotten long ago. I was sure I was the only one who remembered that night. It was such a precious memory. I've never told anyone else.'

'But Mamma—'

He checked himself. He'd been about to remind her that she'd told him about that first evening, but just in time a warning shrieked in his brain and held him silent.

Sometimes the best and kindest thing is to let people believe what they want to believe, whether it's true or not.

She was there again, in his head, in his heart, in the air around him: invisible but now seemingly a permanent presence in his life, saving him from disaster. Saving his mother from misery.

Varushka was regarding him fondly. 'All this time you never really believed that he loves me, did you? But I always knew. When you meet the right one—the only one—there can be no doubts.'

'It must be a wonderful feeling,' he murmured with a touch of wistfulness.

'Oh yes. And it makes me so sad that you've never known that joy. Mind you, I did think at one time that you'd found the perfect girl. You seemed so right together, but then...I don't know...'

'It just didn't happen, Mamma,' he said edgily. 'Let's not talk about her. She's in the past.'

'But it will happen one day. You'll meet someone who seems at first just like everyone else. But then you'll find that your heart is mysteriously open to her in a way that's never happened before. You'll tell her things you've never told anyone else in the world, because suddenly that's what you want to do. And you'll know that hers is opening to you.'

'Will I know that?' Leonid murmured.

'Oh yes. Or perhaps you'll only hope it. Things don't always become apparent at first. It can take time to work matters out, but if she's the one you mustn't give up. And you will know, my darling, because there'll be this little voice inside you saying, "This one is different".'

'Different,' he murmured. 'Yes, there's no hiding from it.'

'That's true and you must always remember it. Never

give up. I never gave up, and now I'm being proved victorious. The day when Amos and I will finally be together is drawing closer all the time.'

'Mamma—'

'Oh, I know you don't want me to hope for too much. You're a realist, my darling. Of course you are. How else could you control that powerful business, and stride the world in the way your father does? I see that side of him in you and it warms my heart. But you've inherited something else from Amos. You have his great heart, the heart that can love a woman endlessly through thick and thin, love her with power and generosity, pinning your life on the belief that one day you will be together, finally and forever. That wonderful aspect of him is also in you, and it fills me with joy. Don't you understand that?'

'I'm not sure…I mean…if I…one moment, Mamma. I think I see something out there—'

Leonid rose swiftly and went to the window, staring out at the garden. His words were a pretence. He'd seen nothing. It had been a frantic device to turn away from her so that she couldn't see his face, filled with emotion and even the threat of tears.

He would die before letting anyone see those tears, even his mother—the only person who could provoke them. Nothing would change her conviction that one day Amos would come to her, and with all his heart he longed to be able to make that happen. He hated himself for his failure, but he could think of no way around it.

She came to join him, understanding. 'Miracles do happen, my dear,' she said gently.

He forced himself under control, giving her a bright smile. 'Yes, sometimes they do,' he agreed.

'And yours will come in time. You'll recognise it at

once. Maybe not at once, but she'll take up residence in your heart and simply refuse to go away.'

'Even if I tell her to?'

'Even then. In fact the more you tell her to, the more she matters. And the more she'll dig in stubbornly.'

'You make her sound like an annoying little pest,' he managed to say humorously.

'Well, it'll take an annoying pest to get the better of you.'

'That's my mother's opinion, is it?' he asked wryly.

'Who else knows you so well?' she teased.

That was true, he reflected. Despite the need for so much pretence with her, she still knew him because she saw a part of him that nobody else suspected, and could say to him what nobody else would dare.

Except the annoying pest, he reflected.

She squeezed his arm.

'I hope it happens to you soon, my dear boy. I want you to be happy, and I know that somewhere there's a woman who can give you that joy. She may be waiting, or you may already have met her and not realised. But she's the only one. Oh my dear, don't fight it.'

'You think I would?'

'I know you. On the day you realise how deeply you love her, you'll run a mile. You resist people, resist trusting them, because part of you believes they'll betray that trust.'

'A lot of people do,' he said ironically.

'But she won't. Whoever she is—if she's the special one she won't betray you. You must remember that, and always be ready.'

'Yes,' he murmured. 'I think I know that now.' He reached for her. 'Come here.'

Gathering her in his arms, he pressed her head against his shoulder, then rested his own head on her hair. That the mother whom he spent his life protecting from reality should have spoken to him with such wisdom touched his heart. He wondered what she would say if she met his 'annoying pest' and the desire grew in him to see them together.

Faintly he heard a long sigh break from her.

'Are you all right, Mamma?'

'Yes. I'm just happy.'

'That's all that matters. Let's go in. You've been out a long time and you're probably tired.'

Together they strolled back to the house. There Nina took over, helping her lie down on the sofa and only leaving her when she was safely dozing.

'How has she been?' Leonid asked when Nina joined him in the kitchen.

'It's hard to say. Sometimes she's seemed agitated, sometimes peacefully happy. She would talk about when you returned, bringing your father with you. I was so afraid of how she'd suffer when he didn't come, but she seems all right now. Thank goodness his letter comforted her.'

'Yes, that's a blessing.'

'Perhaps that's hope for the future. If he's found the way to say things that help her—who knows?'

'I don't think we can rely on that,' he said heavily.

'Oh, I'm sorry. I expect you wrote it really, didn't you?'

'No,' he said quietly. 'It wasn't me.'

'I suppose you have to be off to Moscow to catch up with business.'

'I'm afraid so,' he said heavily. 'I'll stay here as long as I can, perhaps a couple of days, but I should get back to the business soon.'

'The world is full of enemies,' Nina said wryly.

'That's true, but...sometimes I think maybe there aren't as many as I feared.'

She surveyed him with the frankness of one who was a trusted friend as well as an employee.

'You? Letting down the defences?' she queried.

He smiled. 'Sometimes too many defences can do as much damage as too few. You never know.'

She stared at him. '*You* said that?'

'No,' he said hastily. 'I didn't say anything. I must hurry. I have work to do.'

Soon it would be time for the TopGo award ceremony. For Travis, with four nominations, it would be a big night. Also for his family, whom Perdita guessed would gather in Los Angeles, ready to cheer him on and enjoy being together. And Leonid would be there.

She tried to turn her thoughts away from him. She had a living to earn. Returning from the wedding in Paris without a story wasn't what she'd planned for. Her previous success had made her prosperous. She could afford to relax for a while, but she badly wanted to keep her mind occupied.

'Perhaps you should chase after Elizen,' a friend told her over a drink one night.

'Who on earth is Elizen?'

'A psychic with contacts in another world, so he claims.'

'Oh yeah?'

'People swear by him. Some of his successful predictions have been hard to explain but rumour says he's got spies out there who find out things for him, which he then pretends to know by "divine inspiration".'

'Sounds fascinating,' Perdita mused. 'Perhaps it's time I had my fortune told.'

Her meeting with Elizen confirmed all her worst suspicions. He was dressed to resemble a wizard, with a long white beard and a hoarse voice. He went through a performance of reading her mind and made various pronouncements about her life and personality. None of them were exactly wrong, but they were vague in a way that could apply to most people.

Someone who wanted to believe this impostor could be easily fooled, she thought. She made a polite speech, and rose to leave.

'Wait!' he cried. 'Another inspiration has come to me. You're approaching a big decision in your life. You must choose which way to turn, and the consequences of that choice will be with you always.'

'I'll remember,' she said. 'Goodbye.'

Driving home, she mulled it over, wryly amused.

Who does he think he's kidding? He didn't say a thing about me that he couldn't have said about anyone. Approaching a big decision, am I? Me and the rest of the human race. It's time I looked for a more promising story.

When she reached home there was an email from Leonid.

I had to write to say how deeply grateful I am, he wrote. *The letter made my mother weep with happiness, which is all down to you.*

She wished he would have voiced his feelings more, but the rest of the email was unrevealing, and she guessed this wasn't a place where he would display emotion.

Or was there such a place? And, if so, when and how would she find it?

She wrote back warmly, and received a friendly reply. But Leonid's armour of restraint was still in place. She must wait for their next meeting to find more than friendliness.

One afternoon Gary called her.

'Have I got a job for you!' he exclaimed. 'Brazen Bob is in town.'

This was a film star with a big reputation, not only for starring in major films but for his colourful love life and his lack of manners. Brazen Bob wasn't his real name, but everyone agreed that it fitted.

'He's renting a house in London,' Gary said, 'and hiring staff to attend to his needs. Well, we all know what they are. If you get along there fast you could be hired, and then you'll have a bird's eye view. You can look all over the house, discover his secrets.'

'I…I don't think so,' she hedged. 'It sounds a bit sneaky.'

'Sure, and if he was a decent bloke I wouldn't suggest it, but he isn't.'

That was true. Brazen Bob seemed to think that his handsome looks freed him for every kind of low behaviour. At one time Perdita would have pursued him with a clear conscience. But now something had changed.

'I don't think I can,' she said. 'I'm a bit busy at the moment.'

'What else are you working on? Is a big scoop about to land on my desk?'

'It'll take a while,' she hedged. 'I need a bit of time.'

'Hmm. All right, but you'd better come up with something soon if you still want people to think of you as the brightest and the best. I just don't know what's happened to you these days.'

He hung up.

Neither do I, she thought. *Or maybe I do know. Then again, maybe I'd better bide my time, and find out.*

She had said that her heart had never been broken, making the claim partly as a joke. But increasingly she realised that it was true. Thomas, who'd dumped her for fear of vulgar notoriety, and Frank, who'd grabbed what he could and run; they had hurt her pride rather than her heart.

But now, she thought, *now—how can I tell?*

One corner of her mind was annoyed with herself for turning down the chance of a lively story because it would have called for concealment. But her brief time with Leonid had planted a little seed of unease that was now flowering into something that threatened to make life difficult.

It had started in the first moments when she was apologising for spilling his drink by landing on him, and he'd said, 'Don't worry. Accidents happen. It's not as if you fell on purpose.'

The slight guilt from that moment had never quite left her. And now it seemed to be changing her life.

'Oh heck!' she said, reaching for the phone and dialling Gary's number. 'So I'd have to act a bit "iffy". So what, he'll never know.'

But I'd know.

Gary's voice reached her. 'Hi, Perdy, is that you? Fantastic that you called me back so soon. You've decided to do it after all. That's great.'

'No, I…I'm sorry, Gary. I pressed the redial button by accident. Just a mistake.'

'Now, look—'

'Gotta go now. Goodbye!'

'Perdy—'

'Goodbye.' She laid the phone down and sat looking at it before whispering again, 'Goodbye.'

Somehow she knew she was bidding farewell to more than a man, more than a job, more than a way of life.

She was saying goodbye to her one-time self. And doing so for a vague future in which everything was uncertain and confusing.

It was risky.

But she was going to do it.

Suddenly Elizen seemed to be there with her, whispering, *You're approaching a big decision in your life. You must choose which way to turn, and the consequences of that choice will be with you always.*

I'm getting paranoid, she told herself wildly. *He's a shyster. He didn't know about this. He didn't mean anything.*

Again she stretched out her hand to call Gary and agree to do the job. But it fell back into her lap and lay there, refusing to move, and she knew she wasn't going to make the call.

Over the next few days she wondered what the future held if her normal method of earning a living was hampered. Crazily, it was Gary who came to the rescue.

'I don't know why I'm doing this,' he said on the phone, 'but I've been talking to Lily Folles. Remember her?'

'I should think I do. One of the biggest film stars going.'

'Yes, well, she's going to do an autobiography, if she can find a good ghost writer. She remembers you from an interview you did. She liked it, and she liked you. Said you had a sympathetic ear. Here's her number. Just try it and see what happens.'

He hung up without waiting for her reply.

At first she refused to believe that luck could be so much on her side, but she dialled the number, just in case. Lily was thrilled to hear from her.

Over dinner next day they settled it, and Perdita got to work, thanking a kindly fate for sending her a job that she could do openly and without concealing secrets.

It was the step in the right direction that she had longed for. Soon would come the day when she could tell Leonid everything about her career—her past career, as she now thought of it—and their meeting.

For the next few weeks she devoted herself to the book,

spending her life interviewing Lily, or at the computer where Leonid's emails reached her. They were not passionate documents, but they buzzed with something unspoken, something written between the lines.

The award ceremony was being held at the grandiose Felsted Cinema, next to which was the Felsted Hotel, a luxury establishment, and the place of choice for anyone attending the awards. This was where they would both stay, with him taking care of the booking.

I can arrange my own booking, she protested online.

His reply was short and to the point. *No need, I've taken care of it.*

By the same post her booking arrived. Leonid had left nothing to chance.

'Another woman might think you were a bit of a dictator,' she murmured. 'But I guess I'll just have to put up with you.'

Since Los Angeles was eight hours behind London and the flight lasted nearly eleven hours, it was going to be a tiring journey. Nor did she like flying at any time. But Leonid would be waiting at the other end, and that was the only thing that mattered.

She worked until the last minute, cramming in one more interview with Lily, with her packed bags waiting by the door.

But suddenly luck turned against her. Lily had turned up some old memories that she simply had to explain before she too departed for a few days. Perdita kept giving frantic glances to the clock, until even the self-centred Lily noticed.

'Am I keeping you from your flight?' she asked.

'I really should be going,' Perdita said.

'All right, just one more thing. Did I tell you—?'

It was an hour before she made her escape, and even

before she reached the airport she knew it was too late. She was right.

'I can get you a seat on the next one,' a sympathetic steward told her. 'It leaves at ten o'clock tonight.'

Sitting in the café, she sent Leonid an email explaining that she had missed the plane and would not land until the early hours of the morning.

He replied politely. *Thank you for letting me know. Someone will meet your flight.*

She supposed she couldn't blame him for not being effusive. He was probably glad of the delay. Suddenly he had extra hours to spend with his family, or making business contacts.

Yes, she thought, business. He would use the time making money and, being an efficient man, he would certainly remember to send someone to meet her.

It was dark when they landed. There below her were the glittering lights of the city, growing closer. Where was he now? What was he doing? Who was he with?

It seemed to take forever to get through Customs, and she stood looking around, feeling suddenly abandoned. She closed her eyes and shook her head, trying not to believe it, wishing she could simply lie down and go to sleep.

A brief touch on her lips startled her.

'*Leonid!* Oh, thank goodness you're here!'

She kissed him back with fervour, and they stayed like that until somebody asked them to move because they were blocking the way.

'Weren't you expecting me?' he asked when he could speak.

'I thought you'd send someone else.'

'I couldn't put off the moment when we were together. I've been so afraid you'd miss that plane too.'

And he had been, she could see. Behind the steel visor he showed the world was a face that could show doubt and suffering so readily that he kept it hidden.

Except to her.

'I was afraid as well,' she said. 'I didn't really think I'd find you here. But you are, and now everything's all right.'

'Yes,' he said, 'everything's all right. And it always will be—as long as you're with me.'

He put his arm around her and drew her to the exit while a man in a chauffeur's uniform carried her bags. Once in the car he pulled her fiercely against him, refusing to let her go until they reached the hotel.

There he waited patiently while she checked in, then came up in the elevator with her. Now everything about him seemed quiet and controlled, yet the air seemed to vibrate with intensity.

Suddenly he turned and she almost gasped at the burning look in his eyes. Then it was gone. The doors opened, he was leading her to her room, opening the door, dismissing the porter.

As soon as they were alone he sat her down in a chair and pulled back the covers on the bed. Now she was only vaguely aware of his actions. Time lag and the long, extended journey were catching up with her, forcing her to sleep, despite efforts to stay awake. Here she was, alone in a bedroom with Leonid. His fingers were fumbling at her buttons. This had happened before, within a few minutes of their first meeting. Then he'd removed only a little clothing, but now he was going deeper and the next move was inevitable. He would take her to bed and they would make love.

One by one her clothes vanished until she wore only a slip and panties. With tender hands he drew the slip over her head, then picked her up and laid her in the bed.

Half awake, she waited for the feel of his hands caressing her flesh in many places, but he only drew the covers up to her chin, dropped a kiss on her forehead and sat on the edge of the bed, watching her with possessive eyes.

'Leonid,' she said woozily.

'Hush now. Time to sleep.'

She wanted to argue but the clouds were engulfing her brain, drawing her irresistibly into another place.

He leaned close enough to whisper in her ear.

'Can you hear me? No, I'm sure you can't. Or maybe you're just too clever to tell me. I know how clever you can be. I should be more wary, shouldn't I? But I don't want to be wary of you. I want to be close to you. I want to hold you against my heart, and be held against yours.

'Can you understand why I couldn't make love to you? It's because I want to so much. Far too much to seize this moment when you're not really yourself. If I took advantage of you now it would mean nothing. Certainly nothing to you, and how could it mean anything to me, knowing that you were oblivious?

'If—when—we make love, it must be something we share, and remember together, not me grasping what I can get and you unable to remember anything. But I can be patient, for I know our time will come. I don't know when or how it will come, but I see two figures standing on the road ahead. They are gazing joyfully at each other because they have reached the place where they belong. Who are they? Why, they are us, of course.'

He brushed his lips against her mouth.

'Goodnight,' he whispered. 'Until tomorrow.'

He released her and retreated slowly, going through

the door backwards, his eyes fixed on her until the last moment.

Perdita heard the soft noise of the door closing, and snuggled down in bed. She was smiling.

CHAPTER SIX

WHEN SHE AWOKE she lay trying to decide which of her thoughts were memories and which fantasies. One thing she knew. Leonid had removed her clothes until she was almost naked, but had stopped there. He could have done anything, knowing that she couldn't prevent him. But he had resisted temptation.

Unless there had been no temptation. Had he found her so easy to resist?

She seemed to hear his voice speaking in her mind.

'If—when—we make love, it must be something we share.'

Had he said those words? Had he meant them? Confused by longing, she lay reliving the precious moments. Or perhaps only imagining them? She would know soon. The answer would be in his eyes when they met today.

Turning her head on the pillow, she saw him sitting there.

'Hello,' he said.

'Hello.'

She tried to understand what she saw in his eyes, but was baffled. They were tender but mysterious. She wanted to know more. She wanted to know everything.

'Did I imagine what happened?' she asked.

'No. You were dead on your feet and you needed sleep desperately.'

'Was that…all that happened?'

'Yes,' he said, understanding her at once. 'When we take things further it's got to be something we both want.'

'Yes,' she said. 'Yes.' She rubbed her eyes. 'Oh dear, I don't know where I am, what I'm doing or anything that's happening. Have I slept long?'

'Yes, it's nearly midday.'

'Are the rest of the family here?'

'Not yet, but soon. Travis lives in Los Angeles so he won't be staying in this hotel. Marcel will be here later today, so will Darius and Jackson.'

'And your father?'

'He's coming. He wouldn't miss it for anything. He used to look down on Travis as "only an actor", but now he's reaching the big time, Father is impressed.'

'That must make Travis very happy.'

'It means the world to him. Let me get you something to eat.'

While they waited for the food she went into the bathroom to shower. Her heart was singing.

As they settled down to eat he said, 'I have to admit it. I've missed you so much it scared me. I told myself I had work to do.'

'And I was spoiling your concentration, huh?'

'Definitely. I tried to put you out of my mind but—you won't leave.'

'No, I'm an awkward character. I always was.'

'Me too. Everybody says so.'

'I'll second that,' she said lightly. 'But I appreciate that to you I'm just a nuisance. I can go away if you prefer.'

He laid his hand over her wrist with a touch that was gentle yet unbreakable.

'Don't even think of it,' he said. 'I'm not letting you go.'

'So I'm your prisoner?'

'You'd better believe it.'

Their eyes met and she knew that despite his assertive words it was she who was the stronger. This stern man was not in control, although he would die before admitting it.

'Then I won't argue,' she said lightly, touching his cheek.

He smiled and released her.

Again she had the mysterious sense of having landed in a universe where nothing was familiar. In one sense she had known this man for several weeks, but all but three days had been spent apart, communicating at a distance. So how well could she really know him?

And yet she felt she could see the depths of his heart.

'How is your mother?' she asked.

'Well. Happy, *thanks to you.* The letter—well, I told you, didn't I? It pleased her, just as you said it would. She was so happy that he seemed to remember that night. She didn't remember telling me about it, so she thinks the memory comes from him.'

'And you didn't tell her the truth?'

'No, I didn't tell her. It would have been cruel. You were right about that. You were right about everything.'

He took her hand again, holding it gently between his own. His eyes, too, were gentle, sending her a silent message. He'd lived in her heart ever since their parting. Now she knew that she had lived in his heart, and his own efforts to banish her had been equally hopeless.

She had a sudden sense that Leonid was on the verge of saying something, like a man standing on the edge of a cliff, trying to find the nerve to jump. But almost at once she sensed him stepping back, delaying the crucial moment.

'How did you manage to miss the plane?' he asked with a casual air.

'Work demands descended on me without warning,' she said. 'A book I'm writing needed some extra material.'

'You write books?' He looked up quickly.

'Sometimes,' she said, choosing her words carefully. 'Have you heard of Lily Folles?'

'She's a big film star, isn't she?'

'That's right. She's writing her autobiography. At least, officially she's writing it. Actually I'm doing the writing bit. We talk, I set it down, she signs it.'

Under the table she was crossing her fingers. This was her chance to acquaint him with the respectable side of her work, and she was seizing every moment.

'How did you get the job?' he asked.

'I heard that she was looking for someone, I applied. We got along well, and she hired me.'

'Naturally impressed by your stunning talents as a writer.'

'Actually I don't think it was that at all.' She dropped Her voice to a tone of conspiracy. 'When we had lunch—' she looked over her shoulders on each side before saying theatrically, *'I laughed at her jokes.'*

'Oh well, that settled it!'

'I've done several interviews for the book, but she wanted an extra one yesterday. I squeezed it in, and it just went on and on. I couldn't make her stop, and by the time I got away it was too late for the plane.'

'Well, you're here,' he said. 'That's what matters.'

She had a sense of triumph at having drawn him closer to the reality of her career. He knew now that she was a writer with show business connections, but in a more respectable way than her old self. And since that self was being sidelined she felt she was bringing things under control. Problem solved.

'I expect you're wondering how I got into your room this morning,' Leonid said.

She was taken aback. It hadn't occurred to her to wonder. It had seemed so natural.

'The fact is I bribed the porter,' he admitted. 'My room is next door, but I wanted to be able to get in and out in case you needed me. I looked in several times, but I didn't awaken you. You were sleeping like a baby.'

'Well, I'm all the better for it,' she said. 'Refreshed and ready for anything.'

'Anything?' he asked, without looking at her.

'Anything,' she assured him.

Now he turned his gaze on her, and there was something in his eyes that she'd longed to see—warmth, brilliance, hope and, above all, intent. It was that intent most of all that made her heart beat faster as he reached for her.

'Leonid! Leonid, are you there?'

The cry came from the corridor, repeated again and again by several voices.

'Oh no!' Leonid groaned. 'If ever I was sorry to have brothers—*Grr!*'

From outside came the sound of pounding on a door.

'That's my room,' he said. 'I'd better stop them before they get us all thrown out.' He went and opened the door, yelling, 'All right! That's enough!'

Perdita heard yells of delight. Following him out, she saw Darius, Jackson and Marcel. They remembered her from Paris and greeted her joyously.

'We just got here,' Darius said. 'They said you were upstairs, so here we are.'

Harriet appeared, embracing Perdita and saying, 'Let's all go for a coffee.'

On the way down, Perdita said, 'Any sign of Travis?'

'No, I've been trying to call him,' Jackson said. 'I'm a bit concerned. He doesn't answer the landline and his cellphone is switched off.'

But then his own phone rang. He answered it and they all saw his expression change to one of outrage.

'You're where? Why? Well, I'm sorry for Charlene, but—Travis, wait—hang on a minute!'

He addressed the others.

'He's gone mad. Charlene has to dash back to England to see her sick grandmother, and he's taking her to the airport.'

'Will he return here in time?' Marcel demanded.

'He will if he comes right back,' Jackson said tensely. 'Travis, listen to me, you can't seriously mean to go to England—Travis—*Travis*—he's hung up.'

'But he'll hurry back,' Marcel said.

Perdita found her mind dancing back to Paris when she'd seen Travis and Charlene together, and had known by instinct that they were united by true love. She would have found it hard to say exactly how she knew, but the journalist part of her mind had watched them knowingly, observing things that others would never have noticed.

'He'll be back,' Marcel repeated. 'He's not going to miss tonight.'

'Yes, he will,' Perdita said suddenly. 'He'll miss it for Charlene. You don't think he'll let her go alone, do you? He loves her too much for that.'

They all turned to stare at her.

'Enough to miss the biggest night of his career?' Jackson queried.

'Enough even for that,' Perdita said.

'But he just said he was taking her to the airport,' Jackson pointed out. 'He didn't say anything about going with her.'

'Maybe he hasn't told Charlene that he's going to sacrifice himself for her,' Perdita said. 'Otherwise she might decide to sacrifice herself for him. Isn't that what people do when they're in love?'

'But—the awards,' Jackson said. 'Tonight means the world to him.'

'No,' Perdita said. 'Charlene means the world to him. You've only got to watch them together to see the truth.'

She strolled slowly away and went out to sit in the sun, knowing that Leonid would follow her.

'You really mean that?' he said, coming to sit beside her.

'He won't let her down, no matter what it costs him. I guess you think he's crazy?'

'No, I'd understand if that's what he does. But I don't think he will.'

'We'll just have to wait and see.'

'Hey, you two!'

They looked up to see Darius hurrying out of the building.

'Travis has called again, this time to say he won't be here tonight,' he gasped. 'He's just about to board the plane with Charlene.' He turned to Perdita. 'You were right all the time.'

'Yes, she was,' Leonid murmured.

'I've told him I'll explain to the others, including Father, when he arrives.'

'I think he's here now,' Leonid said, and they looked up to see Amos storming towards them, followed by Marcel and Jackson.

'Is this true?' he shouted. 'What Jackson's just told me—that Travis won't be here tonight?'

'Charlene has to go to England,' Leonid said. 'And he has to go with her.'

'Of course he doesn't have to. It's not his problem.'

'He loves her,' Perdita said simply. 'If he lets her down, and loses her, *that* will be his problem, a big one that he'll never recover from.'

'Sentimental twaddle!' Amos snapped. 'No woman is that important.'

He'd been drinking or he wouldn't have spoken so in front of his sons. To Perdita's eyes, the looks the young men exchanged spoke volumes. They knew what kind of a man their father was, and they understood the need for them to be in alliance, if necessary, against him.

'You don't mean that,' Darius said coldly.

Amos scowled but, before he could say anything, his own cellphone rang. It soon became clear that it was Travis, calling from the airport, where he was about to board the plane.

'Have you gone mad?' Amos shouted into the phone.

Faintly they could make out Travis's voice at the other end, but his words only increased Amos's temper.

'You've insulted me. What kind of a fool do I look now, turning up to see you win prizes and you can't be bothered to be here? I'm telling you, no woman is worth it—'

There was a click. Amos stared at the phone, trying to believe what had happened.

'He hung up on me! Can you believe that? He's worked long and hard to get this far and now he'll throw it away to please a girl.'

'But he need not be throwing it away,' Perdita said.

'Of course he is,' Amos snapped. 'If he doesn't turn up everyone will be insulted.'

'Not when they know why,' she persisted. 'Present it to the audience in the right way and he'll be a romantic hero, a man generous enough to put his love first and himself second. His standing will soar.'

'You're right,' Jackson said. 'Listen to her, everyone. She knows what she's talking about.'

Perdita stole a glance at Leonid. He didn't speak, but he nodded and smiled.

'We'd better go and prepare for whatever the night will bring,' Jackson said. 'Disaster or triumph.'

Leonid came upstairs with her.

'You're not as surprised as the rest of us,' he said. 'How did you know? Are you psychic?'

'Maybe. It was just something I sensed about them right from the start. Whenever he held her left hand he'd look down and stroke the ring finger as though he had marriage in mind. Apart from that, it was just there in the way they smiled at each other. If the love is real, you can't hide it.'

'You know, sometimes you're actually a bit scary,' he said. 'The way you can look into people's hearts and know what they're thinking and feeling.'

'Only some people,' she told him. 'Others are good at hiding it—if they want to be.'

He coloured slightly. 'Sometimes you have to be.'

She nodded. 'That's true. Perhaps we should go and get ready now. It'll soon be time for the awards.'

When the great moment came, it was as Perdita had predicted. The Master of Ceremonies announced that Travis couldn't be with them and explained why, and the applause was deafening. It was even more enthusiastic when he actually won one of the four prizes for which he'd been nominated.

'If only he could have been here to collect it,' Jackson

mourned at the family party afterwards. 'How can he bear to lose that moment?'

'He hasn't lost anything,' Leonid said. 'He's simply found something that means more.'

Perdita nodded. 'If the love is that great, then you'll do anything to prove it, no matter how difficult, no matter the lengths you have to go to, no matter what may happen afterwards.'

He didn't reply in words, but he nodded and took her arm.

'I expect you're still tired,' he murmured. 'You ought to return to bed.'

'I think you're right,' she said. 'Let's go.'

Once in her room, he locked the door and pulled her to him for a kiss that was unlike any they had shared before. It wasn't clear which of them moved to the bed first, but they arrived together and lay in each other's arms, brooding, wondering, even doubting a little. Had it finally arrived, the moment to which everything had been building since she'd landed at his feet in Paris?

They lay with their hearts beating together. When he moved she responded willingly. At the supreme moment he looked deep into her eyes, asking a silent question. She answered it equally silently, caressing him in a way that reassured him of the truth of her answer, sighing with delight as he moved against her, responding with all her heart and all her body.

After excitement came peace, lying together in contented joy, each knowing that at this moment there was nowhere else in the world they wanted to be.

Once Travis and Charlene had decided to take the plunge they arranged matters quickly, setting the date for the following month.

'Are you sure you've got the day correct?' Leonid asked as they said goodbye at the airport. 'You won't let work get in the way and make you late.'

'I promise,' she told him for the hundredth time. 'Now hurry. Your flight leaves before mine. Don't miss it.'

Reluctantly he left, turning at the last minute for a final look at her before vanishing into the tunnel on the way to the Moscow flight. She stood there for a long time after he'd gone, feeling that the world was terribly empty.

In the month that followed, all her thoughts and feelings were concentrated on him. Her research had told her much about the man the world thought it knew; a man who'd made his fortune from steel, and maintained a steely control on his life. But she had seen beyond steel to another man who sheltered deep inside him: cautious, vulnerable, lonely. She'd had tantalising glimpses of this other self, leaving her eager to reach out, find him, draw him towards her.

If he'll let me, she mused. *But he must. I'll* make *him let me.*

As before, their emails were mostly impersonal. Leonid's dictatorial side caused him to book the hotel rooms, and pay her bill in advance without consulting her.

'I'm going to have words with you,' she murmured. 'You've got to stop taking over.'

At last the great day arrived when Perdita could return to Los Angeles, and Leonid. He was at the airport, arms open to her. His embrace was so fierce that she gasped, but she was hugging him with equal force.

'I was afraid you wouldn't come,' he said hoarsely.

'You said that last time,' she protested. 'Do you know me so little that you still doubt?'

'Sometimes I think I know you very well. And sometimes I don't feel that I know you at all.'

'That will change.'

'Promise. Promise that your heart is open to me and always will be.'

She took his face between her hands and kissed him briefly but tenderly.

'I promise,' she said. 'Trust me.'

'I do. I always will.'

'Let's get out of here,' she said.

On the way into the city, in the taxi, he said, 'There's going to be a big family party tonight. We have to be there.'

'Of course. Has everyone arrived?'

'Now that you're here, yes.' He sighed. 'We're going to have very little chance to be alone.'

He was right. Everyone had arrived, including Amos, and the next few hours were filled with family celebrations, which drifted to a close only when Travis said, 'Charlene and I must go home now. We have a big appointment tomorrow.' He wrinkled his brow dramatically. 'If only I could remember what it was.'

The others roared with laughter.

'Be careful,' Jackson said, pointing at Charlene. 'She's going to make you suffer for that.'

'No, I just thought I'd vanish without a trace,' she teased.

'But that would be the worst suffering,' Travis said, putting his arms around her. 'Now, let's get home where I can keep a firm eye on you.'

There was more laughter and cheers as the family followed the happy couple out into the street and waved them off.

'She's perfect for Travis,' Jackson observed as they went back inside. 'She doesn't stand for his nonsense.'

'And that's what a man needs in his wife,' Darius

agreed, giving his own wife, Harriet, a conspiratorial look that she returned at once.

That was one of the things that made a happy marriage, Perdita thought: a mutual need that they both recognised and welcomed. Cassie and Marcel were also smiling at each other in a way that excluded the rest of the world.

The same thought seemed to have occurred to Amos, because he was glancing back and forth between Leonid and Jackson to see if either of them was sending out signals to Freya. But Jackson was searching for something in his pocket, and Leonid was looking at Perdita.

'Are you all right?' he asked, for she had closed her eyes.

'Just a bit of jet lag.'

'Of course, you had a long flight. I'll take you upstairs.'

At her door he paused expectantly, a question in his eyes.

'Are you really sleepy?' he asked.

'What do you think?' she chuckled. 'That was just for them. Come in. I have something for you.'

Once inside, she reached into her bag and handed him an envelope. 'It's the money for my bill here,' she said. 'I told you I'd pay it myself.'

He looked inside at the international cheque, then folded it and put it into an inner pocket.

'I'll wait until I'm alone before I tear it up,' he said. 'After all, I don't want you inflicting "terrible vengeance" on me.'

'Are you becoming afraid of me?'

'I could be.'

'Good. That's how I like it.'

'I guess we have a lot of ground to make up,' he said.

She brushed his mouth with her own, increasing the pressure until she felt his arms go around her, drawing her down so that they were both lying on the bed. His lips moved, caressing her, inciting her, commanding, pleading. Tremors of delight shook her and she increased the urgency of her movements.

'You didn't really think I was sleepy, did you?' she whispered. 'I only said it so that we could get away.'

'That's what I hoped. Do you want to stop now? I warn you, this is your last chance.'

'I guess I'll just have to go on then. Lead the way.'

Everything was lovely; the way his kisses and caresses gave and took at the same time; the feeling that she was following his wishes while he was also following hers. She sighed blissfully, wishing it could last for ever.

When they were finished he held her quietly for a moment before kissing her goodnight and slipping out of the room.

Suddenly being alone was unbearable, as though she was isolated, not just in the room but in the whole world. She closed her eyes and tried to sleep, but the sense of desolation was dreadful.

Next day they gathered at the wedding. Watching Charlene approach down the aisle, seeing the look of adoration that Travis gave her, Perdita knew she had been right about them all the time. They had come to the place where they belonged, just as she and Leonid were approaching the same place.

At the reception she saw little of him. He made a speech that drew applause, and raised his champagne glass to salute the bride and groom. More speeches followed. Then the reception gradually turned into a party that would last all evening, and at last he drifted to her side, accompanied by Freya.

'Help, help!' she murmured. 'Amos is trying to throw

me into Leonid's arms when he isn't trying to throw me into Jackson's. Honestly, I'm getting dizzy from being bounced around between them.'

'Well, you stick with me,' Perdita said. 'I'll protect you.'

'Cheers.' They clinked champagne glasses.

Marcel and Cassie joined them, and there was more clinking.

'That was quite a speech Father made,' Marcel said. 'Considering that he's as mad as fire about the wedding.'

'Well, he shouldn't be,' Perdita said. 'They're a lovely couple.'

On the far side of the room Travis was speaking quietly to Leonid.

'I'm glad you brought her with you. She's what you need.'

Leonid gave a wry smile. 'How would you know that?'

'Because I know you better than you know yourself. She'll never gaze worshipfully up at you and tell you you're wonderful.'

'Because I'm not wonderful,' Leonid said with a grin. 'I don't need my brother to tell me that.'

'Nice to see you being realistic. But I meant that she's a strong woman, intelligent and shrewd. You don't believe me now, but in the end you'll find she's been one step ahead of you all the time. What's more, you'll be glad of it. OK, shake your head. You'll find out. Let me tell you something. Do you know the moment when I realised Charlene was different from all other women?

'It was our first evening together. We went to a dinner in a Los Angeles hotel. It was a big public event and some people were surprised I was there because there had recently been some damaging stories about me in the press. They were put there by a man called Frank Brenton, because quite simply he wanted to ruin me.

'When we arrived, Brenton came over, all false smiles and threats. I tried ignoring him, but Charlene faced him down. She told him she always believed the worst of everyone, leaving him in no doubt that she meant him. He escaped fast.

'I could hardly believe what I'd seen, the way she'd charged into battle for me, and flattened the enemy.'

'You really must be in love to say such things,' Leonid said with a wry smile. '"Flattened the enemy". This is a woman you're talking about, a beautiful, delicate woman.'

'Yes, it sounds odd, doesn't it? We're supposed to be the fighters, defending women. Not watching them defend us. But that's what happened, and nothing was ever quite the same again.

'I told her there and then that meeting her was the best thing that had ever happened to me, but it wasn't until later that I realised just how true it was. I meant she was my friend, comrade, someone who'd fight beside me to the end. The love came later, and I understood that the woman you love needs to be your best friend as well. That's when it really works perfectly.'

'If you say so,' Leonid told him. 'As long as it works for you.'

'All right, I understand that look you're giving me. You can skip the patronising older brother stuff. Right this minute I'm the elder because I know something you don't. The day will come when Perdita will take up the cudgels for you, and you'll thank heaven for it.' He gave Leonid a brotherly thump on the shoulder and said significantly, 'Just wait and see.'

CHAPTER SEVEN

TRAVIS MOVED ON, leaving Leonid deep in thought. He didn't take his brother's words too seriously. Seeing Charlene in this light had clearly worked for Travis, but it could never be right for himself. His own instinct was to defend and protect his lady, as a man was supposed to do, not seek for her to protect him.

It was time for the bride and groom to leave on their honeymoon. Everyone waved them off, then returned to the party. Amos exerted himself to draw Leonid and Freya into the same conversation, which they both endured for a while before making their escape.

'For goodness' sake,' Freya muttered in Perdita's ear, 'get your claws into Leonid and run off with him before I do something desperate.'

'Get my claws into him?' Perdita echoed, chuckling. 'Shame on you.'

'Anything you like. Just get him out of here.'

'Ah, I see. Thus leaving you to concentrate on Jackson.'

Freya gave her a glowering look. 'Not him either. Actually, I've got another man in my sights. I may even be announcing my engagement soon.'

'Thanks for the warning,' Leonid said, appearing behind her. 'Remind me to duck before you make the announcement. Bye, Freya.'

Taking Perdita's arm, he drew her out of the room.

'Phew!' she said.

'You may well say phew!'

'Is something the matter?' she asked. 'I saw you talking to Travis earlier and it seemed to disturb you.'

'It was nothing,' he said hastily. 'One thing that does disturb me is that I have to get another letter from my father, and I'm hoping for your help. After the one you wrote, I had to do another one for him, following your methods.'

'Wonderful! You see, you don't need me.'

'Is that what you really think?' he asked. 'Or what you want to think?'

'I don't know,' she admitted. 'You never really know where the road leads, do you?'

'No, especially when there are so many roads leading in different directions. And they seem to criss-cross each other.

'So that it's easy to lose your way,' she murmured. 'Or forget where you intended to be, so you don't even know where that was.'

'Or change your mind about it,' he said.

'Yes, that can be the most confusing of all.'

'The fact is—there's something else as well as a letter.'

He hesitated, and she had the feeling he was struggling inside himself, not even sure that he wanted to say this.

'What is it?' she asked.

'Well—'

'Leonid, you can't stop there. Tell me, please. The suspense is killing me.'

He took a deep breath. 'Will you come to Russia with me?'

She drew in a sharp breath. To be wanted by him was more than she'd dared to hope, but suddenly all the confused criss-cross roads they'd spoken of seemed to whirl before her.

'But I can't,' she said.

He groaned. 'I knew you'd refuse me. Right, that's it! Forget it!'

'No, I only mean that I can't come right now. I need to get a visa first, which means returning to England to make the application.'

She knew this, having researched the possibility a week ago, hoping that he would ask her. But it would be better for him not to know that just yet.

'I'd forgotten about the visa,' Leonid groaned.

'How should you remember? You never need one. I'll apply as soon as I get home.'

'You mean—you'll come?'

'If you want me.'

'If I want you?' He stared as though unable to believe she'd really asked that. *'If I want you?'*

He looked deep into her eyes.

'Yes, I want you. I want—' he seemed to struggle for words '—I want everything. Say yes.'

'Yes,' she said.

'Promise?'

But what did that mean? What would she be promising? Where did the road lead from here?

She didn't care. Wherever that road led, nothing mattered to her at this moment but to travel it with him.

'I promise,' she said.

He leaned towards her, but drew back as they heard people coming closer.

'Let's get out of here,' she said.

Once inside her room they threw themselves into each other's arms for the kiss they had both yearned for, and for which they were both on edge. Her head was swimming from the feel of him, powerful yet tender. He seemed to hold her with a force that could have defied the world, but would be mysteriously unable to defy her.

'We must arrange your trip soon,' he said. 'I can't face all those weeks without you.'

'Hush, don't think of it. Not yet. Just now, there's something else—'

'Yes,' he said. 'There is.'

This time there was no doubt or hesitation. Before she knew it, she was lying on the bed, clasped against his body. His face hovered above hers, intense, purposeful, yet still full of a question. Everything in her responded, *Yes.*

She caressed him, letting him know how willing and eager she was for his loving. He was skilled, but it wasn't his skill that delighted her. It was his tenderness, his care for her, culminating in the most beautiful moment of her life. The sadness came when his body withdrew from hers, but she promised herself that soon, very soon, she would claim him again. And it would not be just his body that she claimed.

Later that night she lay awake, watching him lying beside her, holding her arm with one hand, as though afraid she would vanish while he slept.

'It's all right,' she murmured. 'I'm not going anywhere.'

He muttered something, pressing his face closer against her, and she stroked his hair until she fell asleep.

Next morning he came in while she was packing.

'Look,' he said, 'why don't we—?'

He stopped short, nearly tripping over a canvas bag on the floor.

'I'm sorry,' she said, 'I shouldn't have left it there.'

Quickly she gathered up the books that had slid out. Leonid stared at them in astonishment.

'"A Philosophical Reflection on Ornithology,"' he recited. '"Rational and Irrational Theories on Luminosity."'

'If you could see your face—' she laughed '—it shows exactly what you're thinking.'

'And what do you imagine I'm thinking?'

'Whatever is this stupid woman doing with philosophical volumes? How could she possibly understand them?'

'I've never thought you stupid,' he said, reddening slightly.

'But you don't think I can understand long words,' she challenged. 'Go on, admit it.'

'I've never pretended to understand you. Every time we meet I discover a new side of you that I never dreamed of before. And this—' He indicated the books, then paused, struck by something.

'Professor Angus Hanson,' he read. 'Hanson? A relative?'

'My father. And the one next to it was written by my brother. They've just been published. They sent them to me and, like a dutiful daughter, I started to read them on the plane over here. But don't worry. I don't understand them any more than you thought I would.'

'I'm sorry. I didn't mean to insult you, it's just that every moment makes me realise more how little I know about you.'

'You know the bits that matter.'

'Do I? If you're an intellectual I think you should have warned me.'

'So that you could run a mile?'

'Ten miles,' he said with feeling.

'We've never really had a long talk, have we?' she mused. 'There's always been something going on around us, and we haven't had much chance to get to know each other.'

'I seem to remember talking about myself a lot when

we first met. It's listening that I didn't do. But that's going to change. When we're in Moscow you're going to tell me about yourself, what a learned, educated woman you really are.'

'Not in a million years, so you needn't run. My family are like that. They have great brains, go to top universities, then become professors or write learned books. Or both. Even my mother has a first class degree. I'm just not one of them.'

'But it makes no sense. You're not stupid. You're one of the shrewdest, most intelligent people I've ever known. It's almost scary how on the ball you are.'

'Thank you. But the ball I'm on isn't the one they think matters. My mind sort of dances around rather than goes in for the long haul. I'm the only one of the family who didn't go to university.'

'But you became a writer,' he reminded her. 'I'll bet that book you're ghosting will outsell anything your family write.'

'Yes, I don't deny that's nice. At family gatherings I can hold my head up high in a way I couldn't at one time. They know I've succeeded at something.

'But the older ones—my parents—still see me as the one who isn't up to standard. I've never quite fitted, and I never will. Why do you suddenly look like that?'

'For a moment you made me think of my mother. This is so like what she told me. Her parents were teachers, and they were determined she was going to be like them. They taught her English but were always saying she didn't work hard enough at it.'

'You've got to try harder,' she murmured. 'Anyone can learn if they try.'

He stared at her, astonished. 'Is that what they said to you?'

'All the time. Did your grandparents say the same to her?'

'Something very like. She always knew they didn't consider her a credit to them.'

'Oh, how I know that feeling! I think she and I must be soulmates.' She gave him a steady look. 'I'm sure we'd get on well—if that's what you'd like.'

He stared at her as though unable to believe what he'd heard. 'Do you really mean that?'

'I mean it.'

'I can take you to meet her? You mean it?'

'Of course.'

'Oh, if you knew what it would mean to her. She lives such an isolated life because nobody else understands her, especially about this.'

'But do these things still live in her memory after all this time?'

'Yes, because they ruled her life. It was because of my grandparents' language skills that my father came to be staying with them when he went to Russia on that first trip. After he'd gone she worked harder than ever at perfecting her English, because she wanted to be ready for the day he sent for her.'

'Oh no! How sad!'

'Yes, it is. Even today she reads English books so that she'll still be fluent "when the time comes".'

'She still believes the time will come,' Perdita said sadly. 'And you have to pretend to believe the same thing, so as not to hurt her. But can I help? Could I take her some English books? Would she like that?'

'Oh yes, please do. Do anything you want. I know you'll get it right.'

His eagerness touched her heart.

'Poor Leonid,' she said softly. 'However do you cope?'

'By remembering that I'm all she has,' he said simply.

'I do what I can to make her happy. I know it isn't enough, but if she can meet you it will mean so much to her. It's a wonderful idea. You won't change your mind?'

'I promise. As long as it's what you really want.'

'It's what I want,' he assured her.

'When you arrive we'll have to stop-over one night in Moscow and go on to Rostov the next day so that you can meet my mother. I'm longing for that. Then we'll return to Moscow and be together for as long as we can. I'll arrange for my deputy to run the business for a while.'

'Will it be hard for you to take time away?'

'A little. Things are always happening. In fact I have to go back right now. I just heard that there's been some trouble that I must take care of, otherwise I'd have liked to stay here a little longer, maybe persuade you to stay. But once I'm back there I'll do everything I can to make your visit perfect—for both of us. We haven't been together as much as we need to be. A few days here, then nothing, a few days there, then nothing. This time we're going to concentrate on knowing each other properly.'

She nodded ecstatically. He laid his lips on hers, then led her back up to her room. At the door he kissed her, but didn't try to embrace her further. He'd said the time was coming when they wouldn't have to snatch moments, and all her hopes now were on that time.

'Soon,' he whispered. 'Soon.'

Later that morning they left together for the airport.

'It's not for long,' he told her. 'We're going to be together. We *must*. Goodbye—goodbye—goodbye—'

His plane left first. She watched him go until he vanished into the crowd, then turned away with tears in her eyes.

For the next few weeks she worked without pause, hoping to get as much of the book done as possible so that there would be no problem about going to Russia. She wanted to be free to concentrate on Leonid and the new world that was opening to her.

At night she would lie awake, wondering about what was happening to her.

In some ways we've barely met, she thought often. *And yet...and yet...oh, I don't know what to think.*

But you know what you feel, came the answer out of the darkness.

This was unlike their other separations. Now there were sweet phone calls to look forward to, and emails, sometimes several a day. He never used the word love but he said again and again how much he missed her, how she dominated his thoughts.

Once she teasingly wrote, *Perhaps you shouldn't think of me too much. Think of all those business rivals, ready to pounce if they see you distracted.*

He wrote back, *That's a different 'me'. I only let him out for business. You don't want to know him.*

She replied, *Yes, I do. I want to know both of you.*

She waited, intrigued to know how he would reply to that. But his next email was an account of his latest visit to his mother.

I've talked about you, and she's very anxious to meet you. She says that you sound like a lovely person. I told her she was right about that.

It was a long email, warm and inviting, and she read it with pleasure. But no part of it was a reply to her assertion that she wanted to know both sides of him. She guessed he must have overlooked that.

One event that stood out was the wedding of her cousin Sally to Thomas, the man who had briefly courted Perdita for the sake of her family connections, and abandoned her when she chose her career. It was their engagement party she had missed when she'd dashed to Paris, hoping to corner Travis at Marcel's wedding.

At the wedding she sat in a pew close to the front, watching Thomas as he stood waiting for his bride. He seemed calm and untroubled, and she couldn't help remembering Travis waiting for Charlene. Even seen from the rear he had clearly been agitated, as though he'd feared she would vanish at the last moment. When she'd arrived he'd watched her advance down the aisle with worshipful eyes. It had been a lovely sight.

In contrast, Thomas awarded his bride the briefest glance over his shoulder. His eyes showed only satisfaction that everything was going to plan.

So he got what he was aiming for, Perdita thought. *I had a lucky escape.*

At the reception he approached her, smiling with self-satisfaction.

'Nice to see you. I was afraid you might refuse to come.'

'Why should I do that?'

'Well…after we…you know…'

So he thought he'd broken her heart, she mused ironically. Time to give him a lesson in reality.

'After we what?' she asked innocently. 'Have we ever met before?'

His face showed his chagrin. 'Evidently not. Excuse me, I have people to see.'

He slipped away as fast as he could, leaving Perdita inwardly chuckling, and wondering how she had ever found that conceited oaf attractive. But that was before she'd met Leonid, a man who threw all other men into the shade with his dark mystery, ironic humour and, above all, his need of her; a need that she was sure he didn't yet understand, but which she sensed with all her being.

Jane, her elder sister, appeared at her elbow. Of all her family, Jane was the one she felt closest to.

'You look as though you're having fun,' she said. 'You're smiling very mysteriously.'

'Oh, I was just wondering what I ever saw in that twerp.'

'That's no way to speak about the bridegroom.' Jane sounded shocked and amused at the same time.

'Nonsense, I'll bet every wedding has someone who says that about the bridegroom.'

'You're probably right. And if you've met someone else—' She paused significantly, searching her sister's face. 'Not going to tell me?'

'Not a lot to tell, really.'

'Nothing happening between you and that attractive Russian man?'

Perdita stared. 'What do you know about that?'

'I have a friend who specialises in Russian literature. He's acquainted with Leonid, and happened to see you together in Los Angeles.'

'We were both there as wedding guests,' Perdita protested. 'We weren't dating.'

'Sister dear,' Jane said ironically, 'when two people are so alive to each other, it shows, whether they're dating or not. But don't worry. I'll keep my nose out.'

'But I didn't mean that. It's just that even I don't know what's happening. I'm going to visit him in Russia soon, but after that—' She made a helpless gesture.

'After that he'll ask you to marry him, and everything will be settled.'

'If only it was that simple. I don't know if he loves me. I don't even really know if I love him. And where would we live?'

'In Russia, of course. Where else?'

'But what would I do there? Give up my career and be a housewife? Me?'

'No, you'd have to learn how to cook, and I wouldn't bet on that,' Jane said wisely. 'But you could write that book. The one you used to talk about writing.'

'Yes, I remember now I used to feel cross that all the others were cleverer than I was. Then a couple of my cousins managed to get published and I got all cocky and said one day I'd write a book that would make everyone's head spin. Actually, it may be coming true.'

She explained about ghost writing for Lily Folles, and her sister gasped with delight.

'That's wonderful. But you don't have to stop there. You've been about the world so much that you probably have plenty to say on your own account. You're a gifted writer. And you weren't bad at every subject. You're quite good at languages. That could come in useful.'

'For learning Russian, you mean?'

'Possibly. Look, do what you have to do, darling. If Leonid is the one—go for him. Just make sure it's on your own terms.'

'Thanks, Jane. Thanks for everything.'

The two women embraced each other. Perdita turned away, smiling both outwardly and inside. Today she'd received a gift she'd never hoped for, and the world was a nicer place.

As well as emotional support, Jane had given her practical advice. If her relationship with Leonid flourished she would have to join him in Russia and explore other career possibilities.

And, as Jane had reminded her, there were always books to write.

'Thanks, sister dear,' she whispered. 'You really came up trumps.'

* * *

At last Leonid told her everything was ready. He had insisted on arranging all the travel details, booking her into First Class on the flight from London to Moscow's Domodedovo Airport.

She emailed, *I'll refund you the money when I arrive.*

He replied, *Don't be ridiculous.*

She protested, *I'm not a kept woman.*

His answer was blunt. *Then pretend to be. If my business rivals discovered that I couldn't afford a few plane tickets they'd assume I was vulnerable and move in for the kill.*

That evening the phone rang. As soon as she answered he said, 'I was only joking.'

'That's the first time I've ever known you to tell a joke.'

'I seem to be doing a lot of things for the first time. I'll be waiting for you.'

He would meet her at the airport and take her to his home in the heart of the city. The following day they would both fly to Rostov-on-Don Airport, near the country home where his mother lived.

The last few days were filled with hard-pressed work as she struggled to complete all her tasks. *It must be the same for him,* she thought.

She wondered what else was the same. Was he too on edge, tense with longing for the next meeting, for the first glimpse of each other that would tell them everything?

She tried to tell herself to be sensible. Leonid's first priority was his mother's happiness. It would be foolish to forget that. She repeated this to herself many times on the three and a half hour flight from London to Moscow, but nothing could dispel the hope that burned in her, now more than ever after several weeks of separation. Being sensible was no longer important.

It seemed to take an age to get through Customs and Baggage Reclaim. She scanned the crowd, desperate to see him. For a terrible moment she feared that he hadn't come. She was alone in an empty world.

'At last.'

The voice came from just behind her shoulder. There he was, tense and anxious, taking hold of her, gently but with determination, as though he feared she might escape.

'You're here,' he breathed.

'Yes,' she said simply. 'I'm here.'

He drew her against him and they clung together in an embrace that said it all without words. She closed her eyes, shutting out everything but the feeling of him against her.

'Let's go home,' he murmured.

'Yes,' she said, loving him for saying 'home'. 'But wait, my bags have vanished.'

'My chauffeur took them while we were occupied,' he said, smiling.

With his arm around her waist he led her out into the car park, where a man was just closing the boot of the car. He opened the rear door for them.

'This is Igor,' Leonid told her. 'He'll take us home.'

Inside the car he pressed a button that drew up a divider, giving them a kind of privacy.

'I didn't believe it,' he said. 'Not until I saw you. Even then I feared it was only a dream, one I've had before. So often I've seen you coming towards me and reached out my hands to you. But then I awoke and you weren't there.'

'You're wrong,' she whispered. 'I've always been here. Even when you couldn't see me I was haunting you, driving you crazy with my awkward ways.'

'You did it on purpose, huh?'

'Of course. What else?'

They didn't speak again. Even with the divider up they

were aware of Igor. They must be alone in the universe. Only that magnificent aloneness would suffice.

She was vaguely aware that they were travelling deep into the heart of Moscow. Then the car stopped and they were going up in the elevator, accompanied by Igor and her bags. The door to his apartment opened, closed behind them. Now the rest of the world no longer existed.

Silence, while they stood looking at each other with an intensity that crossed time and space. Then—

'You're here,' Leonid said softly. 'You're here—and you're mine.'

'Yes,' she said. 'All yours.'

CHAPTER EIGHT

THE NEXT MOMENT she was in his arms, held with a ferocity that might have been frightening, but wasn't because she sensed the vulnerable desperation behind it.

Leonid's breath was coming in hoarse gasps.

'Tell me to stop,' he said. 'Tell me now—or it will be too late.'

'It was always too late,' she murmured. 'It's not our choice any more.'

'It was never our choice,' he agreed as his mouth touched hers. 'Never…never—'

His lips explored hers, caressing, teasing, inciting. But he had no need to incite her. The craving that rose up from her depths was already claiming her completely and now she reached out, wanting also to incite him.

With delight she sensed that his desire was already hers as completely as her desire was his. Every part of her body was newly alive, and she rejoiced at what was to happen. If only it would happen soon—soon—

He was pulling at her clothes, unbuttoning the coat that he hadn't given her time to remove. She helped him, then tossed it aside. His jacket followed it onto the floor, and now she could feel him more intimately through the thin material of his shirt. He too was seizing the chance to explore, letting his hands rove over her shape—breasts, waist, hips—lingering briefly to relish the discovery, then moving on.

She felt herself lifted high, carried away into another room and laid on the bed. She pulled him close so that he lay down beside her, his fingers moving swiftly to open her dress and begin to remove it, while her fingers worked on the buttons of his shirt. They opened easily except for one, which stuck. Driven mad by frustration, she yanked at the material so fiercely that the button came off and went flying, landing on the floor with a tinkle.

She never even heard it. She had no attention now for anything but Leonid, his smooth, muscular chest, his tall body that was lean, powerful and intriguing all at once. His face had a look of fierce intent that might have frightened her, except that she wanted the same as he did, and as much. The only thing she feared was that he might stop.

But there was no chance of that. Under his swiftly moving hands the last of her clothes vanished without trace. He drew back for a brief moment to view her nakedness, as though trying to believe it was really true. Then he dropped his head to caress her breasts with his lips, and shudders of pleasure went through her.

The part of her brain that could still think wondered how she'd lived so long without this delight. She was made for this man, made for this feeling of being loved, desired, wanted. And from now on nothing else would do. She must let him know that, and the best way was to claim him as fervently as he was claiming her.

So she arched against him, running her hands over him with all the skill at her command. When he made her totally his own, she knew he'd received and understood her message.

When it was over they clung together desperately, as though trying not to admit that it could end. Neither of them spoke. Words would not have been possible. Nor were they needed. Fulfilment, astonishment that what had happened had exceeded every hope. These were the thoughts and feelings that possessed them equally, and which sent them blissfully to sleep in each other's arms.

She awoke the next morning to find him sitting beside her on the bed, watching her intensely.

'I've wanted you since the very first moment,' he said.

'So have I, but I didn't realise it at first.'

He nodded. 'Yes, it takes a while to realise that the universe has tilted, and you're not the person you thought you were.'

'Or perhaps there are two of you,' she suggested. 'It's something I've had to come to terms with. There's Erica, my sensible side who does all the right things, and Perdita, the cheeky side who drives people mad. I've asked my-self which one I really am, but the truth is that I'm both.'

'I'm glad of that,' he murmured.

'What about you? What's your other self called?'

'I don't know. I'm not that well acquainted with him. Later, perhaps—when we've been properly introduced.'

'You really don't know him yet?'

'I know a few things about him. He's more impulsive, more understanding. He tries to see life through other people's eyes, and he tells me not to be so suspicious of people.'

'And do you listen to him?'

'Sometimes. Often I tell him to shut up and leave me alone. I know I ought to listen more, but it'll take time be-cause I'm not quite sure of him yet.'

'Perhaps you should dismiss him,' she said lightly. 'You might be better off without him bothering you.'

'You could be right,' he said, matching her tone. He

kissed her. 'Time to get up now. We have a plane to catch this afternoon.'

He rose and left her, suddenly wanting to be alone. Never in his life had he told another person so much about himself, and his need to confide in her had shaken him. Her teasing suggestion that he might be better off without the intrusion of his second self had shaken him because he'd often told himself the same.

But in his heart he knew that the 'other' Leonid, awkward, intrusive, hard for him to cope with, was his greatest hope.

Hope. When had his life last offered hope for anything except money? It was like waking up in a new universe.

He returned to the bed, eager to talk to her.

She was gone.

Nightmare. She'd vanished into the mists like a phantom. She had never been there, and he was the victim of a delusion.

Then he heard singing from the bathroom, and closed his eyes in relief. He must be going crazy to indulge in such thoughts.

'Are you there?' he called.

'Unless you have a crowd of women in your bathroom in the morning,' she called back, laughing.

'Better hurry up. We have to eat breakfast and get to the airport.'

When she emerged a few minutes later she found him examining his shirt with a wry look. She looked around for the button, finally finding it in a corner.

'I'm sorry,' she said. 'I'll sew it back on for you.'

'How are you going to manage that?' he asked, holding up the shirt, revealing a gaping tear.

'Oh, goodness!' she gasped. 'I'm sorry.'

'Don't apologise,' he said softly. 'It's nice to be appreciated.'

She took the shirt from him. 'I'll keep this as a souvenir.'

He nodded. 'Good idea.'

Even as he spoke, he wondered at himself. Had he really made those jokey remarks? Or was it another man with his face?

Then he pulled himself together and everything was forgotten but the need to get ready.

He prepared breakfast himself under her fascinated eyes, and served her with a feeling of triumph. He'd taken her by surprise, and that felt very good.

As they ate she glanced around the apartment, taking in details for the first time. It was the home of a rich man, but there was a touch of austerity even in the expensive furniture and décor.

Suddenly she noticed a photograph on a side table. It showed an attractive young woman with large eyes, long hair falling over her shoulders and a cheeky smile.

'That's my mother,' Leonid said.

'She's lovely. But she looks very young there.'

'She was. That picture was taken when she was twenty-two, and just about to get married.'

She thought of what Leonid had told her about his mother's condition these days, how she lived in a dream world because reality was unbearable. In contrast, the woman in the picture looked strong, clever, ready for anything life could throw at her.

'Of course, I didn't know her in those days,' Leonid said. 'But people who did say she was incredible; not just beautiful but vibrant, brave, up for any challenge.'

'That's what I was thinking,' she said. 'And then fate

struck her down. But she was lucky in you. Not many sons are as generous.'

'What else could I do? I owe her everything.'

'I'm longing to meet her.'

'And I'm longing for it too. Let's go.'

The flight from Moscow to Rostov took an hour and a half. When they were nearly there she said, 'How much does your mother know about me?'

'I've told her that we met at Marcel's wedding, that you fell down the stairs and landed at my feet. And she knows you met Amos.'

'Fine. As long as I don't put my foot in it.'

As the descent began they clasped hands, each knowing how much this meant to the other.

'It's beautiful,' she said, looking out of the window as the Don River came into view.

'Yes, it's a lovely place. The house is on the edge of Rostov, close to the countryside and the river, but the town is there if we need it.'

A car was waiting to take them the few miles to his home. Perdita watched eagerly until he pointed and said, 'There.'

Looking up, she saw a gently sloping hill, with a house at the top, with a woman standing outside it.

'Is that—?'

'Yes, that's Mamma. She's waiting for us. Look, she's seen us.'

The woman was waving with both arms, bouncing in her excitement. Leonid leaned out and waved back at her.

'She's happy,' he said as he drew back.

And her happiness meant all was well, Perdita thought, loving him for his sensitive care. She thought of Hortense telling her about him in Paris, saying, 'People who know him say he's hard as nails. You cross him at your peril.'

They don't know him, she thought. *If only other people saw the side of him that I see.*

But he would hate that, she knew. His sensitivity was something he feared to reveal, even perhaps to herself.

As the car drew up his mother was there, beaming, crying out her joy, seizing Leonid as he left the car and throwing her arms around him. He returned her embrace, squeezing her tightly against him, then giving her a warm smile.

'You came—you came—' she cried.

'Of course I've come,' he said fondly. 'I promised, didn't I? And I promised something else, someone I'd bring to meet you. Look, here she is.'

He indicated Perdita, who was getting out of the car.

'This is Erica, Mamma, the girl I've told you about.'

'Oh yes, yes, you have. In fact I feel I know her already.'

Varushka opened her arms wide in a gesture of eager invitation. Perdita had wondered how she might be greeted, but she hadn't dared hope for this warm welcome. Her heart leapt to respond, and the next moment she was engulfed in Varushka's embrace, happily returning it.

'Let's go inside,' Varushka said, taking her hand.

The emotion of the first few moments had completely absorbed her. Only now did Perdita have a chance to study Varushka and compare her with the young woman she'd seen in the photograph.

She was older, with grey hair, but she still had the slim figure of her youth. Perhaps she was now a little too thin, but her eyes were bright and full of life. Perdita had half expected an invalid but, whatever her mental and emotional problems, she still managed to be full of life.

As they took the path towards the house she managed

a quick glance at the large garden and the building before them. She recalled Leonid saying that this was where Varushka had lived with her parents, and had returned after the split from her husband. In one sense it was still a traditional country house, but it was clear that much work had been done to improve it. In this way he could try to contribute to her comfort.

Inside the house, Varushka introduced her to a plump elderly woman.

'This is Nina, who looks after the house and does most of the cooking.' She gave Perdita a look full of sly fun. 'Except when we have special guests and I do the cooking myself.'

'Mamma is a wonderful cook,' Leonid said. 'Whenever I come here my mouth is watering the whole journey.'

'Nina will show you to your room,' Varushka said, taking Leonid's arm to lead him away.

Her room had every comfort, with a large bed, spacious wardrobe and a TV that Nina showed her how to work.

'I am so glad you're here,' she said as she helped Perdita unpack. 'She has been looking forward to it so much.'

'She seems a lovely person,' Perdita observed.

'She is. There is so much love in her, but she has been treated so cruelly that it is more than she can bear.'

'Have you been with her long?'

'I came to work for her when she married. I have seen all her suffering at the hands of that terrible man.'

'You mean Amos Falcon?'

'Yes, but—oh please, you will not tell Leonid that I said that.'

'No, I promise.'

As they finished unpacking Leonid arrived. Nina slipped away.

At once he took her in his arms for an eager hug.

'It's going wonderfully,' he said. 'She liked you from the first moment.'

'And I like her. The way she welcomed me was so wonderful.'

'She'll like you even more if you praise her cooking.'

'Of course I will. I thought she'd be frail and shaky. It's nice to find her strong and confident.'

'Actually—' he paused uneasily '—the cooking is another of her fantasies. It's really Nina who cooks. Mamma shakes a little seasoning over it and we all pretend that... well...'

'I understand.'

'It keeps her happy,' he said.

'And that's the only thing that matters to you, isn't it?' she said tenderly.

He stroked her face. 'Almost the only thing.'

It was on the tip of her tongue to say, *Almost?* and prolong the magic moment. But from down below came Varushka's voice, calling, 'Supper's ready.'

'Time to go,' he said.

She lifted her bag, checking to make sure that it contained something she was anxious to take with her.

'Is there a problem?' he asked.

'No problem at all. You just wait and see.'

He offered his arm. 'Let's go.'

During the meal Varushka took great care of her, explaining every aspect of the elegant Russian meal, offering her a choice of wines, filling her glass.

'This is borscht,' she said as the soup was laid out. 'We make it with beet and meat.'

It was followed by beef Stroganoff, prepared with cream sauce, and pancakes. Perdita relished it all, declaring truthfully that it was wonderful. Varushka beamed.

Afterwards she showed Perdita into the living room

next door. It was elegantly furnished, with a magnificent view down the hill to the river.

'It's so beautiful here,' Perdita murmured.

'Yes, I'm very lucky,' Varushka agreed.

'You've been so good to me. I'm glad I have something to give you.'

From her bag she took out three books and handed them to her hostess.

'You speak English so well that I know you'll understand these,' she said.

'Hanson!' Varushka exclaimed, looking at the covers. 'You wrote these?'

'No, my father wrote two of them and a cousin wrote the other.'

'And you give them to me? That is so generous of you.'

For the next hour Perdita went through the books with her. Leonid, watching, gave both women his warmest look. It was one of the happiest evenings Perdita could ever remember.

'You sound incredibly learned,' Leonid observed once. 'Erica riding high.'

'But my son,' Varushka said, 'why do you sometimes call her Erica, and sometimes Perdita?'

'I was born Erica,' she explained, 'but my nickname was Perdita because when my father knew my mother was pregnant with me he was so cross he said he'd go to perdition.'

'Perdition?' Varushka queried. 'I do not know all English words. What is that one, please?'

Grinning, Leonid told her, 'It means damnation. Perdita, the child of perdition, is a wicked girl, born of a wicked world.'

Varushka was shocked. 'What a nasty thing to say

about such a lovely person. My dear, are you not very offended?'

'No, it can be quite useful,' she chuckled. 'Erica is staid and serious, and rather boring. When I want to indulge my naughty side I become Perdita.'

'So you are two people,' Varushka exclaimed. 'What fun! Do you change from one to the other very often?'

'Mmm, I have to be careful,' she said, giving Leonid a cheeky look.

'And my son calls you by both names.'

'That's because she confuses me,' Leonid said.

'But which one does he prefer?'

'I'm not really sure,' Perdita said, assuming a comically conspiratorial manner. 'I doubt if even he could tell you. But I think he's a little afraid of Perdita.'

'Good!' Varushka declared triumphantly. 'Keep it that way.'

'When you two ladies have finished shredding me,' Leonid said.

But, although his voice sounded mildly harassed, he was regarding the two of them with delight. Nothing could have pleased him more than to see them get on so well, even if it meant they made fun of him.

Perdita was about to say something when she noticed that Varushka's eyes were closing and her head drooping.

'Time for bed, Mamma,' Leonid said.

'Oh no, I don't want to go to bed yet.' But even as she protested she was nodding off.

'You know the doctor said you must get plenty of rest,' he said. 'Come along. We can have lots of fun tomorrow.'

She gave a vague sleepy smile, and he offered her his arm. She leant on it and they made their way across the hall as Nina appeared and followed them upstairs. Perdita followed too, and received a sleepy wave from Varushka.

'Goodnight, my dear.'

'Goodnight,' she called. 'Sleep well.'

She watched as Leonid led his mother into her room, followed by Nina. Then she went to her own room and waited, wondering when she would see him. Or even if she would see him.

He came to her a few minutes later.

'Is your mother all right?'

'Yes, Nina's putting her to bed. This often happens. For much of the time she's full of life, then she just nods off. It's also why we'll only stay a couple of days. Anything longer would be too tiring for her.'

'As long as she's happy.'

He touched her face gently. 'Thank you,' he said. 'You've been wonderful.'

'I think she's the wonderful one.'

'Giving her those books was brilliant. Mind you—' he cocked his head and regarded her satirically '—now you two get on so well, perhaps I should beware. You might gang up on me.'

'There's no "might" about it.'

'I guessed as much. So perhaps I'd better get my revenge in first.'

'You can try. See how far you get.'

'That's just what I intend to do. Unless you object.'

'No,' she said, putting her arms around him. 'I don't object.'

CHAPTER NINE

IN LATER YEARS, when Perdita looked back over this time she could remember only happiness. Varushka had opened her arms and that was typical of everything else she said or did. The warmth of that moment set the mood for the whole visit. It seemed as if some inner sense told her how close Leonid and Perdita were becoming, and she was welcoming a daughter.

Perdita couldn't help thinking of her own mother, whose affection had always been slightly distant, and whose arms did not open to her with anything like Varushka's eager emotion.

It seemed strange to think that she could have gone all her life without experiencing a mother's embrace, and everything had changed because of a woman she had known such a little time.

Perhaps Leonid also understood the feeling growing between them because he often left them alone together. His excuse was always that he must go online to attend to his business, but as the two women sat in the garden she would see him standing in the window, watching them.

Once he saw her looking and placed a finger over his lips, asking her to say nothing. She nodded, but when she looked back she found that Varushka had also noticed Leonid, and was pleased.

'He has told me how you met,' she said. 'You were at his brother's wedding.'

'In Paris, yes.'

'And the two of you were instantly attracted?'

'Well, he was certainly one of the most handsome men there.'

Varushka laughed. 'He was handsome even as a child,' she said. 'Everyone said so. Wait, there's something I must show you. Come inside.'

Taking Perdita's hand, she led her indoors and went to a cupboard, from which she drew out a large book. It was a photo album, overflowing with pictures. Perdita studied it, fascinated by this new glimpse of Leonid.

There was the young Varushka with her baby in her arms, looking down at him with adoration. There were several similar pictures showing mother and child. In some of them little Leonid had grown from a baby into a toddler and was looking back at her, also adoring. Sometimes his arms were reaching out towards her.

One photograph showed the child Leonid sitting on the lap of a heavily built man, who had his arms around him and was looking at him with pride.

'That was my husband,' Varushka said. 'I dare say Leonid has told you the truth about our family.'

'He has done me the honour of confiding in me,' Perdita said. 'He knew I would understand.'

'Of course. And you know that his real father is Amos Falcon. We met when I was already married, and instantly fell in love. I regretted being unfaithful to my husband, but I had never been in love with him. My parents pressured me into the marriage. I did my best to be a good wife, but when I met Amos we knew at once that we were destined for each other. Sometimes love can be like that, overwhelming you before you have time to think. And then, all in a moment, it's too late.

'It was like that with Amos and me. We were meant to be together, even though we both had other commitments. I had a husband, he had a wife.

But we knew what was happening between us, and one day he asked me how to say "I love you" in Russian. I told him it was *Ya tebya lyublyu*. Then he said it to me and I said it to him. And we knew it would always be true.'

'How beautiful!' Perdita said. Softly she repeated, *'Ya tebya lyublyu'*

'One day you will say it,' Varushka observed. 'Perhaps soon.'

Perdita blushed. 'Perhaps. We can never tell.'

'Oh, I think we can tell sometimes,' Varushka said, patting her hand. 'When it's real, you know by instinct, deep in your heart.'

She turned back to the album.

'For a little while we indulged our love, but then he had to return to his own country. In time Leonid was born, and Dmitri, my husband, was so glad that I didn't know what to do. I hesitated about telling him the child wasn't his, and so time passed. I tried to write to Amos, but my letters never seemed to reach him. I think someone was blocking them. It was a long time before he knew he had a son, and by then Dmitri had grown close to Leonid.'

She reached down for another album, which she laid open before Perdita. It was full of pictures of Dmitri with the little boy he had loved. They were heartbreaking, Perdita thought. There was the child Leonid, with a fresh innocent face: the face of someone who had never known hurt or deception. One picture showed him holding up something that looked like a medal.

'He won that at school,' Varushka said. 'He came top

in an English exam. I encouraged him to learn English as soon as possible, so that when he met his true father they could talk.'

Yet the man bursting with pride was Dmitri, Perdita thought, with no idea of the cruel truth he would soon learn. In picture after picture his love shone towards the little boy he believed was his, and Leonid's face was radiant as he gazed at the man he adored as a father.

'He was a decent man.' Varushka sighed. 'I didn't want to hurt him, but when Amos returned to claim me Dmitri learned the truth, and that broke up our marriage.'

'He came—to claim you?' Perdita asked carefully.

'He'd have liked to take me back to England with him, but we knew he couldn't. He had responsibilities, his wife—'

But was it the same wife? Perdita wondered. Or was he even married? By now she'd learned enough of Amos's activities to know how he casually swapped one woman for another, always to suit his own convenience.

'He's an honourable man and he had to do his duty.' Varushka sighed. 'But we swore our eternal love, and he said he would always support me, and Leonid. And that's what he's done ever since.

'Oh, my dear! If I could only tell you how wonderful it is to be loved by such a man, so generous. We are forced to love at a distance, but because our love is great it can survive anything. He writes me such beautiful letters, and gives them to Leonid to bring to me. I cry when I read them because his heart and soul are there, and it's as though he too is with me. Of course, in a way he's with me all the time, but the feeling is more intense when I read his wonderful words.'

'You're very lucky,' Perdita said. 'I know he's a very

powerful businessman. You don't expect such men to be able to write sensitive letters.'

'Oh yes, you're right. Let me show you some of them. I'd love another woman to see him through my eyes, know how marvellous he is.'

The letters confirmed her worst fears. There were very few, because Amos wrote only when Leonid insisted. The emotion was stilted, and the only mention of love was at the end, when he wrote 'love, Amos' as convention demanded.

As she was going through them, wondering what she could say, she sensed a shadow in the doorway and looked up to find Leonid watching.

'I was just showing dear Perdita the lovely letters your father writes me,' Varushka told him.

'They're very nice,' Perdita said, glancing over them.

But then she paused as she realised the letter in her hand was the one she had advised Leonid about when they'd first met in Paris. It was all there, the memories of their stroll through Taganrog, Tchaikovsky's house.

'Do you see what he says?' Varushka urged. She quoted, *"That memory has lived in my heart ever since. And it will always live, because it was one of the most beautiful moments of my life."*

'When I read that I was so happy that I wept tears of joy. It will always live in his heart as it will always live in mine, until the time when we are finally together.' She turned to Leonid. 'It's a beautiful letter, isn't it?'

'Yes, Mamma, it's beautiful.'

'I'm the luckiest woman in the world to be loved by a man who can open his heart like that.'

'Indeed you are, Mamma,' Leonid said. 'And we never know what beautiful good fortune could be waiting for us around the next corner.'

He was looking at Perdita as he spoke. She glanced back, and neither of them saw Varushka regarding them with pleasure.

'You see what he says about Tchaikovsky,' she said, taking up the letter again. 'I told him that the evening we wandered through Taganrog, and we saw the house. I must take you to see it.'

The next day they all travelled to Taganrog and Perdita was able to see the house where the great composer had visited. There were other great names associated with the town, like Chekhov, the playwright. In fact the whole town struck her as fascinating, and on the journey home she listened to Varushka's gossip with real interest.

Varushka spent the evening immersed in the books Perdita had given her, as eager as a child.

'When are you going to write books?' she demanded.

'In a way I've already started.'

She described her ghost writing arrangement. Varushka was aghast.

'So you do all the work and this Lily Folles takes the credit? Everyone will think she wrote it? Shocking!'

'Well, I will get a little credit, buried deep inside the book.' Perdita chuckled. 'But her name will appear in big letters on the cover, and that's good because if people think she wrote it more of them will buy it.'

'But you can't just do this. You must write your own books too, with your name on them in big letters. Your book will not be like your family's, serious and learned. Perdita will produce works that are fun and fascinating. They will become best-sellers, and Leonid and I will boast that we know you.'

Which nobody else had ever wanted to do, Perdita thought, loving Varushka for her childlike eagerness and her all-embracing generosity.

The visit came to an end all too soon. Next day she began to understand what Leonid had meant about how easily Varushka grew weary. After a couple of days she was nodding off every few minutes.

'We should go,' Leonid murmured. 'I don't want to tire her any more.'

On the day of their departure Varushka hugged Perdita fiercely.

'You will come again,' she said. 'I couldn't bear never to see you again.'

'She will come again, Mamma,' Leonid promised.

'Thank you for everything,' Perdita said. 'Thank you. *Spasibo.*'

'Already you speak Russian!' Varushka cried.

'Well, I learned the word for thank you. *Spasibo.*'

'*Spasibo, spasibo,*' Varushka echoed. 'Until we meet again, dear daughter.'

Perdita wondered if Leonid had heard those last words. He was embracing his mother vigorously, saying goodbye.

As the plane rose she looked out of the window at the receding land.

'We can't see the house,' Leonid told her. 'We're travelling in the other direction.'

'I know. I just wanted a last look at the land, to fix it in my mind.'

'Yes, I'm sorry to leave too. It all went so well. But we'll have a few days alone together in Moscow.'

'Alone together,' she murmured. 'Yes, please.'

She saw the understanding in his eyes, and knew that he too could hardly bear to wait until they landed. After that, everything seemed to happen too slowly. The baggage carousel, the journey to his home filled them with maddening impatience. As soon as they arrived he disconnected the telephone and came towards her with a look of purpose in his eyes. She knew that look. It matched her own.

Their loving was swift, urgent and impatient, full of the silent messages that had danced between them for the last few days. He wanted her, needed her, was desperate without her, and she loved him back with all the passion in her.

When it was over they dozed, but only for a few minutes. Then they awoke and studied each other.

'Are you all right?' he asked. 'Do you need anything?'

'I have everything I need, right here,' she assured him with a luxurious sigh.

She looked at him with her head on one side, a smile of contentment touching her lips. Leonid drew a shaky breath.

'Stay there,' he said quietly. 'Don't move. Just let me look at you.'

He was watching her as if transfixed. A man under a magic spell might have looked as he did, motionless, unable to escape, yet filled with a mysterious peace.

For a long time they regarded each other in silence, because no words could be adequate now. At last he stretched out his hand, a question in his eyes, and she moved forward to take it, so that he could draw her closer.

It was she who kissed him first, brushing his lips with her own, feeling him return the caress, pressing closer so that he could feel her rising desire as she could feel his.

'Don't stop,' he murmured.

His hands were moving over her, drawing the sheet away, tossing it to the floor. Now there was nothing between him and her bare skin, and he gently caressed her.

She gave a long, trembling sigh.

'Don't stop!' she echoed him urgently.

Nothing could have stopped him now. Far from exhausting their desire their previous loving seemed only to have inflamed it. She closed her eyes because she no longer needed to see him. She knew him now. He was part of her as she was part of him. When the moment came she felt the world disappear, and understood that she was part of a new universe, one that she had been born for.

Afterwards they slept again. She awoke first, rose from the bed and went to the window, looking out onto the street, wondering at herself. Leonid's embrace could thrill her, which she loved. But his effect on her was far more than that. There was also the sweet contentment which cast a new, glowing light over the whole world. Excitement came and went, but the warmth and peace that only he could give illuminated her whole life.

Softly she crept back to the bed and lay down beside him, her face close to his. He was lying on his side, his face turned towards her, as tranquil and innocent as a child's.

Why do I love you? she wondered. *Why you and nobody else?*

But she knew the answer. It was because he reached out to her, not only with his heart but with his need. For the first time in her life she felt vitally necessary to someone, and everything in her responded with joyful eagerness.

She edged carefully towards him on the pillow and planted a soft kiss on his face, careful not to awaken him. His lips moved and he seemed to whisper soft words, but she couldn't make them out.

'Hush,' she murmured. 'I'm here. I'll be here as long as you need me. Sleep well, my darling.'

He whispered again, then seemed to sink further into sleep, as though a new peace had descended on him. Perdita slid down the bed so that she could lie beside him, holding him in her arms.

The future was still full of uncertainties. If they were to make a life together they must decide where to live. In his country or hers? So many questions to answer, but none of them mattered beside the glorious feeling that she had come home.

For a couple of days it was pure holiday. Leonid showed her around his city like a guide showing a tourist, and she enjoyed it, fascinated by the dramatic history.

'Why are you looking at me like that?' she asked as they sat over coffee at a restaurant one evening.

'I was just wondering when you're going to start taking notes.'

'Why would I do that?'

'You're a writer. Your impressions might make a wonderful travel book. Who knows what might come out of it?'

'That's true,' she agreed. 'Of course, I'd have to spend a lot of time here.'

'I suppose you would,' he said, as though the idea had never occurred to him. 'I'm sure something could be arranged. Waiter!'

That was his way, she thought. Having dropped the hint he turned his attention elsewhere, leaving her to muse. He wanted her to come back to Moscow, not just for a short visit, but to stay there, at least for a while.

And then?

Then things would work out one way or another. He'd sent her several signals, including that he accepted her present work as a writer. The day was coming when she would be able to tell him the truth about her past career. And when there were no more secrets between them they would have achieved the ultimate union, would be closer even than they were in each other's arms at night.

Nothing was ever quite so simple. She already knew that, but rediscovered it that evening when they returned home. As they left the elevator and approached Leonid's front door they found two men waiting for them. The sight made Leonid give a violent exclamation under his breath.

'When we get inside, go straight into the bedroom,' he told her. 'I'll get rid of them.'

'They look dangerous,' she said.

'Don't worry. They're more afraid of me than I am of them.'

And she could sense that it was true. The men regarded him with eyes that were hostile yet nervous. Once inside the apartment she did as he wanted and vanished, but she could hear the voices raised in argument.

'Pazhalsta,' one of the men was saying.

Among the words she'd learned from Varushka was *pazhalsta*, which meant please. This man was crying it out as though his life depended on it.

'Pazhalsta! Pazhalsta!'

There followed the sound of something crashing to the floor. Worried for Leonid's safety, she opened the door a crack and saw him standing. She drew in a sharp breath at the sight of his face. It was hard, cold, implacable. The men were begging him for something he refused to give. There was no yielding in that face, no kindness or sympathy, but something that came close to cruelty. She backed into the room, quietly closing the door.

He came for her a few minutes later. His cold rage had faded and his face was once more the one she knew.

'Sorry about that. You can come out now.'

'What did those men want?'

'I used to do business with them. They tried to cheat me so I ended the contract. Now they're trying to crawl back in, giving me sob stories. But I don't deal with cheats. They're finished. I need to make some calls. I'll join you later.'

'Actually I'm rather tired. I think I'll have an early night. Don't wake me when you come in.'

'All right.'

He hugged her and came as far as her door. She slipped inside quickly and closed it firmly against him. She needed time alone to think.

She didn't go to sleep but lay listening to his voice through the wall. He was on the phone to someone. From the hard note in his voice she guessed he was describing the evening's events.

She tried to blank out the memory of his face. If those men had tried to cheat him he had every right to drive them off with steely anger. Anyone would have done the same.

Yet the sight haunted her. This was the other side of Leonid: hard, terrifying. She'd barely glimpsed it before but it was as much his true self as the side he showed her. This was the face he turned to his enemies, to those who had harmed him, those he hated.

And it was frightening.

When he came to bed she pretended to be asleep.

At breakfast next morning he was his old self again, warm and smiling. The events of the previous night might never have happened.

'Let's go out and have some fun,' he said.

They settled on Victory Park, where there was a fun-fair. She loved funfairs.

For the next few hours they enjoyed themselves like children. Perdita rejoiced in the feeling that this was a new Leonid, one who came alive only with her.

'Let's go and have something to eat,' he said at last. 'There's a place over there.'

When they'd chosen their snack she leaned back and gave a sigh of satisfaction. 'Oh, I'm enjoying this.'

'Good. Later we'll—' He stopped, staring at some nearby trees.

'What's the matter?' she asked.

'Nothing, I...I'll be back in a moment.'

He walked hurriedly away, just as the waiter arrived, occupying Perdita's attention for a moment. When he'd gone her eyes sought Leonid, but there was so sign of him.

Then she saw movement, half hidden by the trees. At first she couldn't be sure it was him, but what happened next astounded her. A young woman walked out into full view, followed by a man who was speaking to her with fierce intent.

It was Leonid.

He was distraught, arguing passionately, as though his life depended on it. But the young woman was giving as good as she got. She was beautiful, with black hair and dark, dramatic eyes. Perdita could see that even at this distance, for they talked with an almost violent intensity.

He reached for her, grasping her arm. But she shook herself free, then turned and ran from him until she vanished among the trees. At once he followed her, until he too was out of sight.

Perdita sat, aghast, wondering what she could possibly do now. But she knew she didn't have a choice. There was no way that she could sit here, waiting for him to return, tortured by suspicions of something he would never tell her. Driven by an irresistible force, she rose and followed them, making her way through the trees faster and faster until her quarry came into sight.

Leonid had taken hold of the woman again, keeping her a prisoner while he spoke to her in fury. Here the trees grew closer together and Perdita could move close enough to watch them unobserved.

She almost cried out at the intense emotion she saw in

Leonid's face. Anguish, bitterness, rage, misery. No man ever looked at a woman like that unless she was vital to him. And, incredibly, he seemed to be pleading with her.

Whatever he wanted, she was refusing him. Perdita heard her scream, *'Niet! Niet!'* No! No!

Then came his answering cry. 'Antonia—'

At last she managed to get free and ran away, followed by Leonid. Perdita stood frozen, trying not to believe what she had seen, but there was no escape. Leonid, that calm, assured man, who valued control above all other virtues, had been torn apart by an emotion that it was beyond his ability to rein in.

He was almost destroyed by the violence of his feelings. A woman who saw that would know she had him at her feet, that she could do as she liked with him.

Yet she didn't want him. What had she learned about him that made her flee with such determination?

Perdita knew she must escape before he saw her. She forced her unwilling body to move and stumbled back to the café. To her relief, there was no sign of him. She fell into the chair and sat, breathing hard, until she saw him heading back to her, alone now. He mustn't know how much she had seen. She seized the guidebook and buried herself in it, apparently so absorbed that she didn't even look up as he approached.

'Found something interesting?' he asked, sitting beside her.

'Er...what? Oh, it's you. I wondered where you'd vanished to.'

'Just a business contact I happened to see passing.'

But the beautiful Antonia had been no business contact. It was clear she was practically the owner of Leonid's heart and soul.

'Did it work out OK?' she asked lightly. 'A profitable meeting?'

'Business is always profitable,' he observed.

Both his voice and his expression were as unrevealing as stone, and her dread increased. Something terrible had happened to Leonid, and he was shutting her out. The message could not have been clearer.

'Would you mind if I went home?' she asked, touching her forehead. 'I'm getting a headache.'

'I'll take you.'

He was solicitous as he helped her into the car and drove her home, but he didn't offer to come up with her, and she knew in her heart that he was as anxious to get away from her as she was from him.

CHAPTER TEN

THE SILENCE IN the apartment seemed to bellow inside her head as terribly as noise. It was everywhere. There was no escape. Thoughts were helpless against it. She had seen something whose meaning was horribly plain, and no arguments could possibly help.

Why had he brought her to Russia? Whatever he felt for her was nothing beside his feelings for the woman in the park. So why should he go to the trouble of bringing her all this way?

The answer came to her in a thunderclap of horror.

He had a use for her. He believed she could bring his mother some happiness, and for that he would play whatever part was necessary, even if it meant assuming a false passion.

She thought of how they had lain in each other's arms, the way his tenderness had moved her, as desire alone could never do. He'd made her feel that she had his heart, which she'd discovered that she wanted more than anything in the world. It was the greatest happiness she had ever known.

And all the time he was only making use of her.

She nearly screamed aloud in agony. She wanted to cry that it wasn't true. It couldn't be true. The man who had given her such joy, such a feeling of belonging, of having come home to the right place—that man could not have been deceiving her all the time.

She began to shake her head, the movements growing more violent every second.

'No, *no, no!*'

She flung herself down on the bed, but stayed there only a moment. This was the bed where they had lain together, and now she couldn't bear it.

She must get out of here, flee this place before he even returned. She pulled out her suitcase and began to hurl things into it. But after a while she stopped, realising that it couldn't be done this way. They must have one last talk in which the truth was brought out between them. Then she would go and never see him again.

And never think of him again, she vowed. But she knew that was a hollow thought. He would be with her, in her mind and heart, to the end of her days.

She lay down, staring, blank-eyed, at the ceiling. There was no hope of sleep, but perhaps she could deaden thoughts and feelings, at least for a while.

Yet even that was denied her. Every nerve remained sharply alive. She sensed the moment when he arrived home, heard his footsteps pause, and guessed that he'd seen the packed suitcase she'd left out there. The moment had come. There was no way to avoid it any longer. Slowly she struggled to her feet.

'What's this?' he asked as soon as she appeared. 'Why are you packing?'

'I'm leaving. I only stayed to tell you.'

'But why?'

'How can you ask me that? Because of Antonia.'

His sharp intake of breath was like a confirmation of all her worst fears.

'You know nothing about Antonia,' he said with deathly quiet.

'I know you're in love with her. After what I saw today I know all I need to. Yes, I saw you. I followed and saw you together. It was there in your face.'

'And you think you can read my face?'

'You were pleading with her, and she was saying no. You're the last man in the world to plead unless you're driven by a force greater than you are. She has something that you want with all your heart and soul. Can you deny it?'

He was deathly pale. 'No, I can't deny it. But it's not what you believe.' He stared at her, his eyes full of bitterness. 'You imagine you know everything. You think you have the right to judge me and walk out without a word.'

'It's better for both of us if I go.'

'You're not going to go, because I won't let you.'

'Leonid, you can't stop me.'

He didn't answer in words, but he went to the door and turned the key in the lock, then stood there, barring her way.

'You think I can't stop you?' he asked quietly.

'I don't believe you'd keep me a prisoner against my will.'

But he would. She knew that even as she said it. He would impose his will no matter what he had to do.

'You'll stay until you've heard me out,' he said. 'If, when you know the truth, you still want to leave, I won't stop you. I thought you were different from other women, more generous, more understanding, more willing to help a man who needed you. But perhaps I was wrong. If that's how it turns out, we'll part and never think of each other again.'

The desolation in his voice as he said the last words

was like a blow over Perdita's heart. The anger that had possessed her only a moment earlier began to fall apart.

'All right,' she said, struggling with herself. 'I'll hear whatever you want me to, but I don't see…I just can't feel we still belong together. Don't forget I saw you with her, I saw the passion in your face. You're in love with her.'

'No!' he said violently. 'Not now, not ever.'

'You're not—in love with her?'

'No. And I never was. If I had been, it might have been better, but I avoided love and, like the fool I am, I made the mistake of being glad of it.'

'Avoided love?'

'Yes. Right from the moment I began to grow up I thought love was dangerous, that a wise man stayed clear of it, because sooner or later it became rejection.'

'Not always.'

'No, not always. Some are lucky, but some of us come to accept rejection as normal. And then we keep our distance, because it's better to hold back than reach out and risk seeing others turning away.'

'But if you hold back—' she struggled to find the right words '—doesn't that make it more likely—?'

'That they will turn away from you? Yes. You're right. Why do you think I'm still so alone in my life? Because of my own actions.'

He strode away to the window and stood with his back to her, staring out into the night. The sight of that darkness made Perdita's heart ache. She could sense how it confronted him, surrounded him, stifled him, poisoned whatever might bring him comfort. She longed to reach out to him, but instinct told her that the moment had to be right.

The man she knew was warm, generous, reaching out to the world and herself. Superficially, he seemed to have gone, but deep in her heart she knew better. That man was still there, fighting to survive the disasters that would crush him, waiting for her to come to his rescue.

She went to stand behind him, putting her arms about him and leaning her head against him.

'You're wrong about that,' she said. 'What's happened to you isn't your fault, and I'm going to make you understand that. We're all helpless against events that happen without warning, but you don't realise that because you're so powerful in other ways. It's a kind of armour but it can't always work.'

He turned, frowning as he considered her words. 'Shouldn't a man be armoured?'

'Not always. I think perhaps you wear too much armour. Strength that is too great can be a weakness.'

'And you think I'm like that?'

'Do you know, before we ever met, someone warned me to steer clear of you because you were scary.'

'Advice you were too foolish to take,' he said wryly.

'I've dealt with worse than you.'

'Why do I find that so easy to believe?'

'Perhaps because you're beginning to know me. And I'm beginning to know you. You're so powerful that you think you can control everything, and that's sad because it makes you feel to blame for everything. But you're not.'

'He told me I was,' he murmured, seeming to look into the distance at something visible only to him.

'He? You mean Amos?'

'No, I mean Dmitri Tsarev, the man I thought of as my father until I was ten. I adored him, and he loved me.'

'I know. I saw you together in those pictures.'

'My mother didn't want to keep the pictures because he was in them, but I made her. Once I caught her trying to cut him out, so that there was only me. I begged her not to, but even so I don't think she's ever really understood what he meant to me.'

'Yes, it was there in his face,' she remembered. 'And in yours.'

'He used to say no man had ever been so proud of his son. And then Amos returned to Russia. Dmitri learned the truth and he turned on us with hate.'

'He blamed you?' she asked incredulously. 'But how could he?'

'Because he'd given me his heart, and when he found I wasn't really his son I think he went mad. I pleaded with him to tell me what I'd done, but he screamed at me that I was a bastard, evil and a curse on his house. When I tried to put my arms around him he shoved me away.'

Perdita uttered a violent word, making him stare at her.

'I hope he rots in hell,' she said. 'To take it out on a child, the one person who was completely innocent. *Damn him!'*

'He died two years ago. I hadn't seen him for a long time by then. He'd thrown us out of his house and wiped us from his life. I used to write to him, hoping he'd write back.'

'Did he ever?'

'The only time I ever got a response was when he sent my letter back, torn into little pieces. With it was a note saying, *"You are not my son".'*

'Bastard,' Perdita muttered. 'I mean him, not you. What happened after that?'

'Amos gave my mother money, but that was all. He clearly thought money was enough. She tried to make me understand that he was my real father, but everything was at a distance. Anyway, I didn't care. I wanted Dmitri but he rejected me completely.'

'He indulged his own feelings at your expense. You were a child. Did he ever think what he was doing to you?'

'No, because he didn't care.'

'But you said he loved you.'

'Only because he thought I was his son. When he knew I wasn't I stopped existing as far as he was concerned.'

'So he assumed you felt nothing because that was convenient to him. And then you decided it was better to feel nothing.'

'That was when it first occurred to me,' he agreed.

'What about Antonia? Weren't you in love with her?'

'I was attracted to her, we were together for a while, but for some reason I couldn't make the final commitment. I felt there was something missing, and a voice inside my head kept whispering, *There must be more than this.*

'Things came to a head one evening when she kept pestering me to declare more than I felt. I'm not proud of myself. I behaved badly. It turned into a quarrel, and we parted in anger. The next day I tried to contact her to say I was sorry, but her phone was dead. I went to her house but she wasn't there. She'd just vanished.

'A few weeks later I came across her by accident. She was about to marry another man. She was pregnant.'

'Pregnant? You mean—?'

'Yes, with my child.'

'And she hadn't told you?'

'No. I asked her why. I said I'd have married her if I'd known. But she said it wasn't good enough for me to marry her because of the baby. She wanted me to love her, and when she realised that I didn't, she walked out. She said she'd found a man who did love her.

'I begged her to call the wedding off, to marry me instead. I couldn't believe the feelings that shook me at the thought of being a father. I said she had no right to separate me from my child, but she screamed that she wouldn't settle for second best with a man with no heart.

'I was at their wedding. I slipped in at the back and watched them, knowing I was losing something that would have given my life a new purpose. And yet I couldn't blame her. I'd failed her.'

'You're doing it again,' she protested. 'Taking all the blame on yourself.'

'Isn't that where it belongs?'

'Maybe some of it, but not all. You were clumsy, floundering, but that's not a crime. And you paid a heavy price for your mistake. Much heavier than most people pay.'

'Perhaps my mistakes were worse than most people's.'

'Don't say that. You're not to say that or even think it.'

He managed a wry smile. 'It seems I'm not the only one who gives orders.'

'Was that the first time you'd seen Antonia since it happened?'

'No, I was slightly acquainted with Fyodor, her husband. I've managed to put some business his way, and find reasons to drop in on them from time to time.'

'Does he know that you're the father?'

'No, which is ironic really. I'm acting much as Amos did about me, except that I wanted to marry Antonia. I wasn't in love, but I wanted the family I'd never really had. As it is, I have to watch Oleg being reared by another man.

'I remember once I met them in the park, her and Oleg. We were chatting pleasantly. Oleg and I were swapping jokes. It was wonderful. Then suddenly Fyodor appeared. Oleg saw him and yelled "Papa!" He ran and threw himself into his arms and they hugged each other, just as father and son should.'

'That must have been terrible for you.'

'Yes. I suppose I should have known what was bound

to happen. Antonia wants me to stop visiting them completely. She says Oleg is beginning to look like me and Fyodor will start to suspect that he isn't the father.'

He dropped his head into his hands and groaned.

'I know she's right. If Fyodor knows the truth he might reject Oleg as Dmitri rejected me. I can't do that to my son. I know what it's like, and I have to protect him. I only asked her for one more meeting, just Oleg and me, so that I could say goodbye to him. Of course, I wouldn't tell him the reason. I'd invent some excuse, say goodbye, then go away and never trouble them again.

'But she won't even consider it. I'm banished and that's it.'

'Come here,' she said, putting her arms around him and holding him tight. She was wrung with pity.

'You won't go, will you?' he said.

'Not now. I thought it was what you wanted.'

'You thought I'd want to separate? Don't think that for a moment.' His breath came harshly. 'Not you. *Not you.*'

'All right, if you say so.'

'But you don't believe me, do you?'

'I think you're full of confusion about…well, about everything really.'

Love had betrayed him at every turn. The man he'd thought of as a father had turned on him cruelly. His real father valued him only at a distance. Now the son he loved was lost to him. Life had taught him that to yield to love was dangerous, because eventually there was only betrayal. And he had thought she too was about to prove that fear was real.

'I'm going to stay here,' she said, 'whether you want me or not. If you don't want me—too bad. I'm here for life.'

He stared. 'Do you know what you're saying?'

'Yes, I'm saying that I belong to you. If you'll let me,

I'll move in here. Otherwise I'll camp outside until you realise that you can't get rid of me.'

'Don't say that if you don't mean it.' Leonid's voice was shaking.

'I do mean it. I'm yours.'

'Mine,' he repeated slowly. 'You don't know what that means to me.'

'But I do. I know how often you've been let down, but those days are over. Now I belong to you and you belong to me.'

'Do you mean—that you'll marry me?'

'If that's what you want.'

'If that's what I want. Can you even ask? What I want is for you to be there every moment of every day and night. But I want more. I want to know that you'll *always* be there, until the very last moment of my life or yours.'

'And I will. My promise.'

He took her face between his hands. 'Do you understand, you are the one person in the world from whom I would believe such a promise?'

She nodded. She understood exactly what he meant. He was drawn to her not only by love, but by the conviction that she was his one hope, the only person he could cling to in total reliance.

His gaze was still on her face, as though he could fix her there for eternity.

'While I have you the world is good,' he said. 'If ever I should lose you—'

'You never will,' she vowed. 'Never. Never.'

'And you will never lose me. My heart will always be yours. Do with it what you will. It will never want anyone but you. Marry me soon. I want to make sure of you as quickly as possible.'

'That sounds as though you don't really trust me,' she said. 'You still have doubts.'

'It's not you I distrust, but an unkind fate that will try to take you away from me. I don't know how, but it'll try, and I'm not going to let it.'

'We'll fight it together,' she assured him.

He kissed her. 'Mamma will be delighted. Let's go and tell her as soon as possible.'

'Oh yes. Let's do that at once. Is there a plane today?'

There was one in two hours. On their way to the airport, Leonid called his mother.

'Mamma? We're on our way. We'll see you this evening. Something wonderful has happened. No, I won't tell you now. Wait and see. Bye!'

He hung up and turned to look at Perdita. She thought she had never seen so much blissful joy in any man's face, and her heart leapt to know that she was the cause.

There was nothing to warn her of the disaster that was about to descend on them.

CHAPTER ELEVEN

THEY FOUND VARUSHKA waiting at the door, eagerly watching for their arrival.

'Tell me it's true,' she cried, throwing open her arms to them. 'Tell me you're really going to be together.'

'How did you know?' Leonid asked, hugging her.

'I've always known.' She embraced Perdita. 'My dear daughter.'

It was wonderful to be welcomed and drawn into the magic circle, Perdita thought. Now, at last, she had a family.

As they toasted each other in champagne Varushka said, 'Leonid, don't you remember I once told you that you must always be ready for the special one? And you were. I'm so glad.'

She had cooked an elaborate meal in celebration, but she hardly ate anything herself. Most of her attention was taken up watching Perdita from the other side of the table, sighing rapturously.

'You must marry her soon,' she told Leonid as he followed her out into the kitchen later. 'She'll be much in demand.'

'I'm sure she is. She's beautiful.'

'She's also famous. Some men like a famous wife.'

'Famous?' Leonid queried. 'Ah yes, there's the book

she's ghost writing. She certainly knows some famous people. But how did you know?'

'I found her in a newspaper. You know since I learned how to use the Internet I go through a lot of foreign newspapers, to see if there's anything about your father.'

He did know. She only spoke two languages, Russian and English, but she accessed papers in all languages, just looking for his name.

'I was going to show you this anyway,' she said, 'because it's in French so I'll need you to explain it to me.'

'Show me.'

She called up the newspaper and he saw a piece about Amos.

'But where's Perdita?' he said.

'I found her quite by chance. I was just flicking through and came across her picture. I saved it so that you could tell me what it said.'

There on the screen was Perdita, looking a little younger, though undoubtedly her. But what made Leonid grow tense and still was the sight of the man with her.

There was the same man he'd thrown out of the Paris hotel. He was sitting down, with Perdita standing behind him, one hand on his shoulder. It was the most casual contact, but there was no doubt that they were familiar with each other.

Slowly, reluctantly, with gathering disbelief, he translated the French.

...the devastating journalistic team of Frank Binley and Perdita Davis that pulled off a dozen scoops until they broke up...

'What does it say about her?' his mother asked eagerly. 'Nothing much,' he said. 'This was several years ago.'

Perdita, who had stayed behind, now followed them into the office.

'Hello,' she said.

'Perdita, my dear,' Varushka cried, 'I was just showing Leonid a piece about you. Come and look.'

She went forward to gaze at the computer screen, while all about her the world seemed to churn in chaos. It had finally happened, the thing she had dreaded. Leonid would have recognised Frank and immediately understood the rest.

She glanced at his face and shivered. Not because it was angry. But because it was dead.

A man made of stone might have looked out of such blank eyes. She'd last seen those eyes full of passion and warmth.

Now they were dead.

'You must tell me everything it says about you,' Varushka said.

'Of course, Mamma, but not tonight,' Leonid said. 'It's getting late. We'll talk again tomorrow.'

'All right. Oh, I'm so looking forward to it.' She yawned. 'Oh dear. I don't want to be sleepy now.'

'But you must rest,' Leonid said. 'We'll have plenty of time tomorrow. Here's Nina.'

He followed them into Varushka's room, bid his mother goodnight and returned to Perdita. For a while they regarded each other in silence. At last he spoke.

'It's him, isn't it?' he said. 'That slimeball is a friend of yours.'

'Not a friend. We once worked together but it was years ago.'

'You're a journalist, working in cahoots with that man.'

'Not now. It's in the past.'

'But you were both in Paris—'

'That was coincidence. I didn't know he'd be there. I hadn't seen him for years.'

'But you used to work with him, sneaking around, conniving, pretending to be something you weren't, pretending not to be what you were. And that's why you were in Paris. It wasn't an accident that you landed at my feet. You thought I was Travis and you calculated that was a way to get close to him. That was it, wasn't it?'

'Please listen to me—'

'Wasn't it?'

'Yes, but if you'd only let me explain—'

'The last thing I want to hear is your "explanation" of how you played me for a fool. I fell right into the trap, didn't I? I even made it easy for you by asking for your help. I took you everywhere with me, right into the heart of my family. How you must have laughed!'

'No, never,' she snapped, getting angry in her turn. 'Why don't you shut up and let me tell you what really happened?'

Leonid folded his arms and stepped back, regarding her with derision. 'All right, go on. Tell me. I could do with a laugh.'

'It started as you said, but very soon I realised I couldn't go through with it. I got...involved. Don't pretend you don't know what I mean by that. I abandoned all idea of a story. I couldn't do that to you.'

'Oh, please! Don't take me for a fool. Or perhaps I've only myself to blame if you do. I acted like a fool, didn't I? Falling for your wiles so easily. I even let you compose my father's letter. What a brilliant sneaky item you must have thought that would make!'

'No,' she cried passionately. 'I did it for you, because I wanted to help you. Nobody else ever heard a word about it.'

His lips twisted in a wry smile that was almost a sneer. 'I've got to hand it to you. You know all the right things to say. I wonder how often you've said them before. How many other idiots have you deceived with those eyes and that sympathetic manner? That's the real weapon, of course: the soft voice, the sweet expression. So convincing.' His voice became livid with contempt. *'So well practised.'*

'Stop it,' she said fiercely. 'It was nothing like that. I never wrote a word about you, then or since. Yes, I once did show business interviews, and perhaps I broke a few rules to get them. But I gave up after we met. Since then I've done nothing but the Lily Folles book, which she invited me to write. And that's how I'm going to work in the future.'

'And what difference is that supposed to make? You may have changed since but, even if you have, you still contrived our meeting as part of a deception. It makes me sick to think how nice you seemed, how I felt able to reach out to you. And all the time you were ticking boxes in your head. Fooled him with that lie! On to the next.'

'But soon I started to feel bad about it,' she cried. 'I was already beginning to worry about some of the iffy things I had to do, and realised the time had come to change. I meant to tell you, but I couldn't find the right moment. Leonid, we've known each other for three months. In that time have you ever seen a word in print that could have come from me?'

'No, but who knows the story you're planning? You know enough about my family now to make a lot of money.'

'But I won't,' she cried. 'That's all over. You can trust me.'

'Once I thought so too, but a man learns wisdom. I

loved you, I believed in you, I thought you were the one who…well, never mind. It was all based on a fantasy.'

He walked away, leaving her in despair. She had always known the truth would be dangerous, but she had seemed so close to escaping the worst. She'd thought the day was dawning when she could tell him about the past as something that was over long ago and could never touch them.

She would not give up hope. Their love was strong enough to overcome this.

Night was falling. She went out into the garden, seeking Leonid, but he had vanished. After wandering about for an hour, she returned to her room and lay looking into the darkness, wondering if darkness would be all her life contained after this.

At last she heard her door open and close.

'Don't put the light on,' he said.

Full of hope, she held out her arms to him, but he stayed at a distance.

'I've just been to see my mother,' he said. 'I've told her you have to hurry home for family reasons. I'll take you to the airport tomorrow.'

She gasped at this brutal rejection.

'Can't we talk first?' she begged.

'Talking won't change anything. We need a little time apart, to think and feel, and decide what this means to us.'

'I can tell you what it means to me,' she said, speaking softly but with passion. 'I love you. That hasn't changed. I'm still the same person that I was.'

'But who is that person?' he asked. 'I thought I knew her, and I thought I loved her too. She's unlike all other people in the world—more faithful, more loyal and generous. Her heart is open to me, and I can place my faith and trust in her without a moment's hesitation, knowing that she will always be there for me, until the end.'

'Surely if you feel like that—'

'But does she exist? I no longer know the answer to that. Could any woman in the world be as perfect as the one who lives in my heart?'

'Nobody's perfect,' she said passionately. 'I don't pretend to be.'

'Nor I. And perhaps you should beware of me. Why do I make so much of this? Why don't I just say it's in the past? What matters is what we've found together since. Why don't I just brush it aside like that?'

'Because I can't. I can't help what I am. I told you once that I believe love ends in betrayal, and perhaps that makes me unfit to live with.'

'And that means you think I've betrayed you?'

'It means I see betrayal where no other man would see it. My mother said something to me recently that I can't forget. She said if I discovered I was deeply in love with a woman I'd run a mile. And she's right. In that sense I'm a coward, and the best thing you can do is get far away from me.'

'No,' she said passionately. 'The best thing I can do is take your hand and show you the way to the future that we can make together.'

'Don't,' he groaned, dropping his head into his hands. 'Don't tempt me with illusions. Don't love me, don't trust me, don't give your life to me because I'll ruin it.'

'Because after today you'll never completely trust me again?' she asked sadly.

'Because I can never trust myself.'

She rose from the bed and went to stand before him. In the darkness she could barely see him, but the sensation of him towering over her was intense. Her head swam with the awareness. He was so big, so powerful, so frail and vulnerable.

'You have me,' she said. 'I'll never leave you. Even if I have to get on that plane tomorrow, I'll still be here, in your heart, in your mind, in your awareness every moment. You won't be able to send me away, no matter how hard you try.'

She kissed him, feeling him tremble in her arms. His returning kiss was fervent, passionate, almost pleading, but all her senses told her that he wouldn't give in. He was trapped by something too strong for both of them.

She took a step back towards the bed. 'Leonid—'

'Don't,' he begged. 'Just say goodbye. It's the only thing left to say.'

He walked out, closing the door behind him, leaving her once more in darkness.

Next morning Varushka bid her a tearful farewell, making her promise to return soon.

'We'll have an engagement party, and perhaps Amos will be able to come. Oh, I'm so happy.'

'I'm sure we'll all have cause to be happy,' Perdita said, forcing a smile.

At the airport Leonid barely spoke a word until they reached Check-In. Then he looked at her with fierce intensity, and she could have sworn there were tears in his eyes.

'Forgive me,' he whispered. 'I can't explain, I just… can't do anything else. Try to forgive me.'

'Can you forgive *me?*'

'Don't ask me that. I don't blame you but…if only I could make you understand—'

'We'll talk when we see each other again,' she said.

But in her heart she wondered when—or if—that would be. She walked a little distance away, then turned to look back at him. He was still there, watching her. She smiled and blew him a kiss, but he never moved. She headed on to the entrance to the tunnel, and at the last moment she turned back again.

He was still there, but now his head was sunk down between his shoulders in an attitude of total despair.

Eyes blurred with tears, she walked on.

Once back in England, she had more time to brood than she would have chosen. She could feel her heart breaking at the tragedy that engulfed Leonid.

This man who'd ruthlessly achieved wealth and success, untroubled by finer feelings, had bowed his head to her in a manner that was almost submissive. And now the depth of his own love scared him.

Throughout his life, the people he'd loved had rejected him. The man he'd believed to be his father had cruelly thrown him out. His actual father had no true affection to offer.

Varushka's love for him was warm, but she had turned into a needy child, taking everything he offered but with little to give back. By his own admission he'd become a man who backed away from love because he believed that nobody could love him for long. *Reject before you are rejected* had become his motto.

But then *she* had come into his life and everything had seemed to change. Suddenly love and trust were possible, and hope could live for him again. A closeness had sprung up between them so intense that they had both yielded to it. She had opened her arms and her heart to him, and miraculously he had responded with the same depth of feeling. But at the first hint of doubt the bitter lessons of a lifetime had made him retreat.

What touched her most was the generosity that made him blame himself, warning her that he was not a man fit to live with. He was right. He would always be troubled and difficult, but she would willingly take the risk.

If only they could talk about it. She tried his cellphone and waited, heart beating, for the sound of his voice.

But it didn't come. The phone had been switched off.

To reject her? Surely that wasn't possible. He wouldn't go to such lengths even if he had made the deadly decision.

But, with despair, she knew that nothing was impossible. Leonid was a man of inflexible will.

But she too was strong-willed, and she refused to give up so easily. She began to dial his landline at Rostov. This time it was answered quickly, but not by Leonid. It was Nina's voice she heard.

'Nina,' she said. 'Thank goodness. Is he there?'

'Yes, he is here.'

'Can you fetch him, get him to talk to me?'

'No, I…I'm sorry, I can't. He has ordered me not to disturb him for any reason, and I dare not disobey.'

'Why—what's happened?'

'Oh, it's terrible. She is dying, and I think he will die too. He is so heartbroken.'

'Dying? You mean Varushka?'

'Yes, she had a heart attack. He tried to send her to hospital, but she screamed that she didn't want to leave her home. He had to give in, lest her agitation brought on another attack. He has two nurses living here to give her all the attention she needs, but we all know how it must end.'

'Oh Nina, how terrible.'

'I will tell you something even more dreadful. She keeps asking for Amos, but he refuses to come. Leonid was on the phone to him many times, but Amos won't budge. Once he lost his temper and shouted so loudly that even I could hear him from several feet away. He yelled,

"What difference does it make? She's dying. Soon she won't care if I'm there or not".'

'Bastard!' Perdita said furiously.

'Yes. When Leonid turned I could see the tears on his face. He brushed them away but not soon enough. He doesn't like people to know how deeply he feels things, but it's there.'

'I know,' Perdita whispered.

'He'd like to go to Monte Carlo to talk to his father face to face, but he dare not leave in case she dies while he's away. It's destroying him, but there's nothing anyone can do to help him. He stays with her night and day.'

For a moment she nearly begged Nina again to tell Leonid she was on the phone, but she checked herself. One fact was cruelly, blindingly clear. She had no value to him and no power to ease his misery. She was useless.

'Tell him I called,' she pleaded. 'Say my thoughts are with him.'

'I'll tell him,' Nina vowed.

'Try to call me when you get the chance.'

'I will.'

'And please, tell him he's not alone.'

But it wasn't true, she thought wretchedly as she hung up. Leonid was completely alone, with a terrible loneliness that was worse because he'd chosen it himself. He was about to lose the last person he'd allowed himself to love without reservation, and he would face the loss in soul-destroying isolation because he felt safer that way than trusting another human being. Even one who loved him as much as she did.

And so he would go on down the long tunnel that led to the death of his heart, leaving only a steel robot.

Absorbed in these thoughts, she was barely aware of another suspicion creeping up on her. By the time she was alerted to it several weeks had passed, and she was able to be certain.

She was pregnant.

In the first surge of joy she forgot everything except that she was carrying Leonid's baby. When she told him about it everything would be different. All the doubts and troubles between them would vanish because the only thing that mattered was their child. Whatever the future held, that connection would always be there.

But then a dark thought came to her.

That's what she *must have told herself,* she thought. *When Varushka knew she was pregnant with Leonid she believed everything would be all right. She didn't realise that Amos would keep her at a distance.*

And Leonid was Amos's son.

But a different kind of man, she reassured herself. He was more generous and loving, and the tragedies of the years had given him a yearning for a stable family life, which she could now fulfil.

Then she remembered his face as he'd dealt with the two men who had cheated him. Pitiless, unforgiving: the son of Amos Falcon.

Also, he'd fathered a child with Antonia, then with herself. In this way as well, he was the true son of that cruel, tyrannical man.

It seemed the curse of Amos Falcon spread its tentacles far and wide.

'No,' she told herself. '*No!* These are just fantasies It's not his fault. Any day now he'll call me. I must tell him he's to be a father, and this time his child will know him, love him. That will bring us together and wipe out the troubles of the past.'

And if you feel, as Antonia did, that he only wants you because of the child, can you settle for that?

It was a terrible question, but the answer came at once. *Yes, if I have to settle for that, I will. As long as it makes him happy. His happiness is more important than mine.*

'There is no curse of Amos Falcon,' she murmured. 'And if there is, we'll face it together—and defeat it together. Oh, if only he would call me.'

But he didn't, and she realised that she must go to see him in Russia.

'There's no time to waste,' she brooded. 'I must go quickly. If only he doesn't slam the door in my face before I can tell him.'

She went online, found the flights to Rostov and booked one for that evening. Then she went straight to the airport. There were still some hours to wait and she spent them in a small café, drinking tea and wondering what the future held.

'Papers. Anyone want papers?'

A newspaper seller had entered and was making his way around the tables. One of them had a picture of Amos on the front page. She bought it and glanced at the story, which was a fairly meaningless piece of guff about some argument he'd become involved in.

Varushka was dying and all he could think about was arguments with other rich men, she thought grimly.

'Is anyone sitting here?' came a voice from overhead.

'No.' She moved up to make room for a middle-aged man who dumped himself into the seat beside her and scowled at her newspaper.

'Damned Falcons,' he growled. 'Curse the lot.'

'Have they ever harmed you?' she asked.

'Amos Falcon has. Never did an honest day's work in his life.'

'He must have worked hard to build the empire he did,' she observed.

'I never said he didn't work. I said he wasn't honest, any more than any of them big shots are. Why do you think he lives as a tax exile? Because everywhere else he's cheated the taxman and had to get out. Let me tell you...'

He talked for half an hour, and she soon realised that he knew his subject well. He worked in banking, not a powerful man, but someone who understood enough to be a danger to others, if they were only shrewd enough to realise it.

Perdita heard him with a bored look, but she was far from bored. Part of her brain was taking mental notes, but she knew any sign of interest would silence her companion, and nothing on earth was going to make her let this chance slip. It would never come again.

She was standing at a crossroads when her life could be transformed. And not just her own life. But she must play the game carefully if she was to win.

And I'm going to win, she thought. *If it's the last thing that ever happens to me, I'm going to win.*

At last she yawned.

'You must be wrong about Amos Falcon,' she said. 'He couldn't have got away with it all this time—'

'He's good at covering his tracks. Of course, if anyone had known the stuff I've been telling you—but they don't.' He became suddenly remorseful. 'I'm sorry, I shouldn't have gone on about this. It must bore you silly.'

'Not at all,' she said. 'You've no idea how interesting it's been. Well, I must be going now. Bye.'

The airport had free Wi-Fi, so she found a comfortable seat and got straight to work, feeding in scraps of information she'd learned that night, making notes, comparing files, testing ideas. A stranger witnessing her face would have been intrigued. A scientist making an earth-changing discovery might have looked as she did.

At last she strode out, went to a ticket desk and said, 'I need to change my flight. I've booked for Rostov but I need to go to Monte Carlo instead.'

'There's a plane in two hours.'

'I'll take it.'

As she headed for Check-In she paused, looked up high and murmured, *'My time has come. I'm going to win!'*

CHAPTER TWELVE

AMOS FALCON LIKED few things better than to indulge himself in the Casino de Monte Carlo. Here he could test his skill and his luck, both of which were usually kind to him. There were other advantages too, notably young women whose company he could enjoy without answering awkward questions. Janine was an excellent wife, and her greatest virtue was that she left him free to enjoy these evenings alone.

On this particular evening his glance around the luxurious surroundings revealed several females whose company he would enjoy, but also one whose presence confused him.

'I believe we've met before,' he said. 'Miss Hanson?'

'That's right.' Perdita gave him her most engaging smile. There would be time for revelations later. At this moment she wanted to get him off guard.

For the next few minutes she played naïve innocence so well that even Amos was fooled. He bought her champagne and they sat and drank together.

'Ah, this is lovely,' she sighed. 'Just what I needed.'

'I'm surprised to see you here.'

She gave him a conspiratorial look through narrowed eyelids. 'There might be a lot of things that would surprise you,' she murmured.

So she was flirting with him, he thought. Good. That would be a useful weapon to separate her from Leonid. If such a weapon was needed. Rumours of a quarrel between them had reached him, but it was safer to be sure.

'So you're here for a purpose?' he said.

'Oh yes, I'm here for a purpose.'

He gave a knowing smile. 'I begin to feel sorry for your next victim.'

'So you should. Oh yes, when I've finished he's going to wonder what hit him.'

Amos chuckled. 'So tell me. Who's the poor fellow who's going to end up wishing he hadn't been born?'

She gave him a long, slow, spell-binding look.

'You,' she said.

Darkness had fallen and nobody noticed the young woman who walked quietly up to the back door of the house and slipped inside. Only Nina, who let her in, knew she was there.

'I was afraid for you,' she murmured.

'It went well,' Perdita said. 'The driver dropped me at the turning, as we agreed, and there was nobody else on the road.'

Nina seized her in a warm hug. 'Thank you with all my heart for what you're doing. If only it can succeed!'

'Is Amos here yet?'

'No.'

'He should be here soon. He promised. If he breaks his word—well, he'd better not. I can be scary when I'm angry.'

Nina nodded. 'I believe you. And I'm so glad you're on *her* side. You're the only hope she has.'

'Let's pray it works out. How is Leonid?'

'In a terrible state. He won't leave his mother for a moment. He knows she's coming to the end, and he's desperate to find some way to bring her comfort and happiness, so that she can die in peace. But he can't do it.'

'Surely it must give her happiness to have such a devoted son?' Perdita protested.

'Yes, and he tries to believe that. But he knows there's something missing, something it isn't in his power to give. And that knowledge is breaking his heart. If the miracle doesn't happen I think it will be broken for ever.'

'The miracle will happen,' Perdita vowed. 'It must. Wait. Isn't that his voice? He mustn't know I'm here. Where can I hide?'

'In the cupboard behind you.'

Perdita just managed to slip out of sight a split second before Leonid opened the kitchen door, calling, 'She's thirsty, Nina.'

'All right, I'll bring her—'

She stopped as the front doorbell sounded. Hidden in the cupboard, Perdita closed her eyes, hoping for this to be the miracle she'd longed for and which she'd done so much to bring about. She heard footsteps, the front door opening and Leonid's cry of incredulous relief.

'Father!'

There followed a mumble that she could just discern as Amos's voice. She clutched the wall, almost faint with relief, straining to hear as much as possible as they moved across the hall towards Varushka's room.

Nina opened the cupboard door. 'They've gone in,' she said. 'Do you want to see?'

'Can I really?'

'Come with me.'

She led the way out of the house, into the garden, to the place where the trees grew close to the window of Varushka's room. The curtains were drawn back and Perdita could see Varushka lying, propped up by pillows. Leonid was sitting on the bed, holding both her hands in his, smiling and talking to her gently. There was no sign of Amos, and she guessed Leonid was preparing her.

She knew she was right when Varushka's face was suddenly illuminated with joy. Leonid went to the door and ushered Amos inside. At the sight of him Varushka's joy increased wildly. She struggled up from the pillows, reaching forward, crying out, 'Amos, my love, my love. You came to me.'

He sat on the bed, taking her into his arms, almost engulfed by her embrace. She was thin and frail, yet for a moment the violence of her emotion made her the stronger.

At last he laid her back on the pillows, but still she kept hold of him, gazing fervently into his face. Through the half open window Perdita could just hear her.

'I've dreamed of this moment—I knew you would come to me—'

'Well, I am here,' Amos said.

To Perdita he sounded uncomfortable, but she doubted if Varushka would notice. She knew only that he was with her, and her world was full of happiness as she ran her fingertips over his face.

'Dearest love,' she whispered, 'I could never go without saying a last goodbye to you.'

Amos muttered some reply which Perdita couldn't hear, but Varushka still smiled. Then her eyes closed and her hands fell away from Amos. For a moment Perdita feared that she had died, but the rise and fall of her chest confirmed that she had only fallen asleep. Leonid checked and nodded with relief.

Amos was already moving to the door. Leonid followed, calling Nina to take their place and call them if there was any change. Perdita backed quietly away around the side of the house to where she knew Nina had left a door open for her.

Once inside, she saw Leonid take Amos into his office. As expected, he shut the door firmly, but she wasn't going to let herself be excluded. She slipped into the next room and went as close as she dared to the connecting door. She would pick her own moment to tell them she was here, but there were things she needed to know first.

'That happens often,' she heard Leonid say. 'She has so little strength. It deserts her suddenly and the next moment she's asleep. She wakes again soon, but the doctor says she can't have very long, and that's why I'm so grateful to you for coming.'

'Are you saying you're surprised?' came Amos's sharp voice. He sounded angry.

'Well, yes. When we spoke on the phone you said… well, never mind, but you didn't seem inclined to come. I should have realised that you were too generous to deny her last wish. Now she can die peaceful and happy. I can't tell you what it means to me.'

'Don't talk to me like that, you hypocrite,' came Amos's sneering voice. 'You know damned well why I'm here, and it's none of that sentimental stuff.'

'I don't understand you, Father. I asked you to visit her while there was still time. You were kind enough to do so—'

'Yes, because you twisted my arm with threats you should have been ashamed of.'

'Father, I don't know what the hell you're on about.'

'Don't pretend. It was your girlfriend who did the talking, but you were behind it.'

'Girlfriend?' Leonid echoed, sounding bewildered. 'What do you mean?'

'That writer you were stupid enough to get involved

with. Erica—Perdita, whoever she really is. She went muck-raking about me, and she found things that could cause me a lot of trouble. Next thing she turns up in Monte Carlo, telling me to get out here or else she'll expose me.'

'I think you must have gone mad,' Leonid exclaimed. 'You're saying that Perdita came to see you?'

'She was there in the Casino, watching me across the Black Jack table. I couldn't believe it at first, but she came on to me, all smiles. Oh, she was completely at home, set on her nasty little deception.'

'I don't believe it.'

'Don't deny it!' Amos raged. 'Why else would she come, except to please you? She gave me a long list of things that could cause me trouble and made it plain that either I got out here or I'd end up wishing I had. Not only that, but she forbade me—*forbade me*—to contact you about it. She said if I did I'd be sorry. You sent her, and you weren't even man enough to talk to me about it.'

'But I didn't send her. I've had no contact with her for weeks. I don't know what she's doing or where she is.'

'I can tell you that,' Perdita said, appearing from the next room. 'She's here.'

Both men stared as though seeing a ghost.

'You,' Leonid whispered. 'You—at last.'

'Good evening, gentlemen,' she said smoothly. 'Please don't waste time arguing.' She faced Amos. 'Leonid is telling the truth. He knew nothing about this. I told you that when we talked in the Casino.'

'You told me a lot of lies that day,' Amos snapped.

'On the contrary, I told you a lot of truths. That was what you didn't like.'

'You used my son to find dirt about me.'

'No, I've told you Leonid isn't part of this.'

'Not knowingly perhaps, but you played your tricks.'

He turned on Leonid. 'And you just let her wheedle things out of you.'

White-faced, Leonid glared at him. 'She didn't.'

'Believe him,' Perdita said. 'Leonid isn't in thrall to me. To him, I was a passing curiosity. No more. He never loved me and he never will. Nor could I, or anyone else, make him do what he didn't want to.'

She wasn't looking directly at Leonid but she was still acutely aware that her words were affecting him. He was full of tension that was mysteriously different from what had possessed him only a moment ago.

Amos was oblivious. Only his own rage and petulance concerned him.

'Fine talk,' he growled, 'but you don't fool me. Not in thrall to you! I know when a man's off his head about a woman. I saw his eyes follow you everywhere. You could do what you liked with him, and you did. There's no other way you could have known what you did.'

'Nonsense, of course there is,' Perdita said. 'I have my sources, many of them, spread over a wide distance. Leonid knew nothing about it and I didn't want him to know. That's why I stopped you contacting him.'

'Why, you scheming little—'

'Yes, that's right. I scheme and connive and deceive. I pretend, I wear false faces, I use underhand methods that no decent person would think of using. I learn things about people that they don't dream of, and I use that knowledge as I think fit. Don't look so outraged. It's what you've always done yourself.'

'You blackmailed me,' Amos snapped.

'Yes, I did. It was the only way.'

'Now, hand over those files. It's time for you to keep your word.'

'And I will, when you've finished the job.'

'I've done what you wanted. Hand over.'

'No, you haven't finished yet. You still have to go back to Varushka, and keep her happy a while longer.'

'Now, look—'

'No, you look. I'm giving the orders here, not you.' She turned to Leonid. 'When she wakes she should find him sitting there beside her.'

'Listen—' Amos raged.

'She's right,' Leonid said. 'Mamma must believe you never left her side for a moment.'

'This girl's really got you where she wants you,' Amos sneered. 'She says, "Do this, do that!" and you do it.'

'Perhaps that's because she sees things with a clarity I can't match,' Leonid said softly.

He turned to Perdita as he spoke, gesturing for her to go on ahead. As she went into the bedroom, Nina rose from where she sat by the bed and stood back to make room for Amos. No sooner had he sat down than Varushka's eyes opened, gazing directly at him.

'I was afraid you would have gone away,' she whispered. 'Or perhaps that you weren't really here at all. So many times I've thought you were with me, but then I opened my eyes and you were gone.'

Conscious that he was expected to say something, Amos managed, 'Not really. I thought of you a lot.'

He was doing his best, Perdita realised, but he was embarrassed and awkward. He needed help.

'And if he thought of you, he was really here,' she said. 'Just as you thought of him. People who love each other so much are never really apart.'

She gave Amos a small unobtrusive nudge, and he responded on cue.

'Very true. We should always remember that.'

Then Leonid leaned forward to stroke his mother's face

and said gently, 'And I can tell you how much in his heart and mind you've always been. Whenever I've been to see him he speaks of nothing else, asking how you are, if you miss him as much as he misses you.'

That's it! Perdita thought. *You've got the idea. Keep going.*

She couldn't speak the words but they were there in the shining look she gave Leonid. He met her eyes, sending her a message of perfect understanding, and for a moment they were one again. She had the dizzying sensation that he had reached out and clasped her in his arms.

'I've been so lucky,' Varushka murmured. 'I've had the love of the dearest man in the world. Even though we couldn't be together, his love was always there to sustain me.

'In my son too I have been blessed. Dearest Leonid. And Perdita—'

Until then, Perdita hadn't known Varushka had seen her. But now she gave her a warm smile.

'How kind of Leonid to fetch you, dear girl. If you are wise you will seize the chance to make him your husband, for he is like his father, the kindest and most generous of men. Witness what he has done for me, how he helped my dearest Amos to be here.'

'He is the most generous, loving man alive,' Perdita said.

'Yes,' Varushka whispered. 'Yes—both of them. Even through the years apart, I knew I always lived in Amos's heart and one day he would return, however difficult it was.' She pressed Amos's hand. 'Dear Leonid, dear Perdita, I only hope life can bring such joy to you.'

'Perhaps it will,' Perdita said. 'I have something to tell you that I hope will make you all happy. I'm pregnant. Leonid and I are going to have a baby.'

Varushka gave a little cry of joy. Perdita heard her faintly, but she was looking at Leonid, who stared at her, thunderstruck.

'It's true,' she told him.

'We…a child?' he stammered.

'Yes. Our baby. Yours and mine.' She turned back to Varushka. 'And your grandchild.'

'My grandchild,' she murmured. 'And Amos's too.' She turned her head towards him. 'My love, we were always united in our son. Now we are united again in our grandchild.'

'Yes,' he said gruffly.

'United for ever.'

'For ever,' he growled.

Varushka reached up to touch his face. 'Goodbye, my dearest. Goodbye until we meet again. And we will—one day. Thank you for everything.'

She stretched out a hand to touch him. With her other hand she reached out to Leonid, who took hold of it. Both men sat watching as her eyes closed. Gradually her breathing stopped and only her smile remained.

After a silence Amos asked, 'Is she dead?'

'Yes,' Leonid said softly. 'She's dead.'

'Well, that's that then.'

Perdita gave him a look of disgust and took his arm, drawing him away. Leonid must have this moment alone with his mother. At the door she looked back and saw him laying down his head against Varushka's breast.

As he must often have done in his childhood, she thought.

She closed the door firmly to give him privacy.

Back in the office, she handed over the papers to Amos, who went through them and grunted. After a few minutes Leonid joined them.

'Is this everything?' Amos demanded, indicating the papers.

'Everything,' Perdita confirmed. 'But you don't have to worry. If you'd refused to come I'd never have published a word.'

'What?'

'I wouldn't have done anything that could hurt Leonid, but I guessed you wouldn't realise that.'

'I suppose you think you've been very clever,' Amos snapped. 'That silly story about a baby—'

'It was the truth, although I suppose I shouldn't be surprised that you didn't understand.'

'Are you saying that you're really—?'

'Yes. Your grandchild—and Varushka's, so you won't be able to forget her existence, the way you were planning to. Whenever you look at the child you'll remember her. I'll make sure of that.'

Amos muttered something that sounded like a curse, glaring at them both with equal hostility. 'Right, I'll be going. You won't need me now.'

'Thank you for coming,' Leonid said quietly. 'It meant everything to her.'

'Call your driver and get him to take me to the airport.'

Leonid did so, keeping one hand on Perdita's shoulder as if fearful that she might escape. But she had no intention of leaving.

'Goodbye, Father,' he said at last.

It was clear that Amos couldn't wait to escape, and cared for nothing else.

They saw him to the car and watched as it drove away into the darkness. Leonid didn't speak, but he drew her back into the house, then into Varushka's room. She was still smiling with the air of peace, contentment and fulfilment that had come to her at the end.

'Thank you,' he said quietly. 'And yet that doesn't begin to say what I want to. There are no words to thank you for what you did for her. It took so much courage to stand up to Amos. Such a risk for you to take. And you did it all for her.'

'Not for her,' Perdita said at once. 'For you. I knew what it would mean to you, and nothing else mattered. I would never have published a word about Amos. Please believe me.'

'I do,' he said fervently. 'I believe you, and I always will. I even believe—*can* I believe that we are to have a child?'

'Yes. Your child and mine. Believe that and believe this. I love you. I shall always love you, and I shall always stay with you—if that's what you want.'

'It will always be what I want,' Leonid declared fiercely. 'I ask myself why you should doubt it. But I know the answer. Because you know I'm a coward.'

'No, don't say that.'

'It's true. For years I've avoided love. I thought a man was stronger without it, but he isn't. He's weaker. I lacked the courage to face up to love, welcome it into my life, take its risks. When I saw you off at the airport I felt that my life was over, but I still couldn't call you back. I wanted to but I seemed to be paralysed. It makes me a man that no woman in her right mind should love.'

'But where you're concerned I'm not in my right mind,' she said. 'I guess I never have been, and never will be. It's true about the risks, but I'm willing to take them because the rewards are so beautiful that they turn it into a new world.'

'Our world,' he murmured. 'The one we can make to-gether—'

'And explore together, and we'll find so many things we never dreamed of.'

'I remember something you said once, something that's lived with me ever since. When Travis missed the award ceremony for Charlene, you said, "If the love is that great, then you'll do anything to prove it, no matter how difficult, no matter the lengths you have to go to, no matter what may happen afterwards."'

'That's right. I had to get here to tell your mother about the child before she died, and make Amos come too, to give her that happiness. Because I knew what it would mean to you to see them together, joined in the knowledge of their grandchild.'

'I've never dared to believe in such love,' he murmured.

'Believe in it now. It's real and it will always be real. Listen to me. *Ya tebya lyublyu.*'

He smiled. 'You're already speaking my language.'

'Varushka taught me the words.'

'Ya tebya lyublyu,' he repeated. 'Yes. Always. But think of the sacrifices you'll have to make to marry me. We can't live in different countries—'

'Of course not. I'll have to come and live here, and concentrate on writing books. That's what *she* wanted me to do, and I think she saw a great deal.'

'She wanted us to be together,' he murmured.

'Yes. Look at the way she's smiling, almost as though she was giving us her blessing.'

They both leaned down and gently kissed Varushka's cheeks, then backed out of the room, closing the door quietly behind them.

Leonid led the way to the living room. There he took her in his arms for a kiss whose tenderness conveyed the overwhelming relief he'd felt from the moment he'd seen her. For a long time they stood, holding each other with love and reassurance.

'I can't believe you came back to me,' he murmured. 'I've longed for that. Every day I'd yearn to see you appear out of the blue, making the world right again. But I knew I had no right to hope. Can you forgive me?'

'Have you forgiven me for deceiving you?'

'You didn't really deceive me; perhaps just a little at the beginning, but you changed. You told me that, and I know it's true. By the time I found out, so many things had happened between us that I should have just relegated it to the past. But somehow I couldn't. At least, not then. Now everything is different.'

'I know. Truly, I do understand.'

'Yes, because you can look into my heart and mind, and read everything there. Aren't you frightened by what you see? The weakness, the confusion, the uncertainty: a man who doesn't know what he's doing?'

'A man who needs me,' she said.

He nodded. 'Yes,' he said. *'Yes.'*

In her heart she knew that the resolution of their love would be no 'happy ever after'. He was a troubled man and he always would be. But she could give him something nobody else could give, and his need for her would never die.

'Yes,' she repeated. 'It won't always be peaceful. We'll fight—'

He nodded. 'Yes, we will. Mostly you'll win, but sometimes—' he gave her a smile that was both warm and wry '—sometimes you'll be kind enough to let me win.'

'I'll think about it. But I'll always be here for you,' she said. 'I've promised that before, but perhaps now I can make you believe it's true. Whatever goes wrong, we'll defeat it together.'

Suddenly Leonid grew very still as a strange sensation came over him. Travis was mysteriously there in his mind as he had been on his wedding day, telling Leonid about the time Charlene had charged into battle for him and flattened the enemy.

She was my friend, comrade, someone who'd fight beside me to the end.

Thinking of how Perdita had stood up to Amos, challenging him without fear, Leonid felt almost dizzy.

The day will come when Perdita will take up the cudgels for you, and you'll thank heaven for it.

'That's right,' Leonid whispered. 'And it's taken me until now to see it.'

'See what?' Perdita asked.

He took her into his arms. 'I'll tell you one day,' he said. 'But there's no hurry. We have all our lives.'

* * * * *

Mills & Boon® Hardback
June 2013

ROMANCE

MEDICAL

Mills & Boon® Large Print

June 2013

ROMANCE

HISTORICAL

MEDICAL

0513 GEN STD LP

Mills & Boon® Hardback

July 2013

ROMANCE

MEDICAL

Mills & Boon® Large Print
July 2013

ROMANCE

HISTORICAL

MEDICAL